Praise for Shearwater Storm

"Wounded by the past, and reluctant to open their hearts again, two souls grapple with love and loss in Arthur Winer's debut novel, *Shearwater Storm*. Set against the incomparable beauty of the Pacific Northwest, a raging storm on a remote island mirrors palpable inner storms the characters face as they make life-altering decisions. Fans of well-crafted love stories will devour this haunting, heart-wrenching, and ultimately hopeful read."

Ashley E. Sweeney, Award-winning Author of *Eliza Waite*

"*Shearwater Storm* is a love story, the love of a woman for a stunning, remote island where she can mend her broken heart, and for the steady life she has created with her husband and son. The unexpected appearance of a handsome, injured sailor awakens a lost part of herself, and as she struggles with her attraction to him, the reader is swept along on her journey to find herself. The landscape of the Pacific Northwest is tenderly rendered, as is Winer's love and respect for the sea. An engrossing read that I thoroughly enjoyed."

Susan Cole, Author of *Holding Fast: A Memoir of Sailing, Love and Loss*

"Arthur Winer's *Shearwater Storm* is a lyrical story of two wounded hearts drawn to each other on a remote island off the coast of Washington state. Winer conveys the setting, as well as intricate details about island life and sailing, with expert knowledge that transports the reader and mesmerizes the senses. A heartfelt, must-read story about love, healing, and the adventure of finding your bliss."

Jan Moran, USA Today Bestselling Author of *Seabreeze Inn*

"*Shearwater Storm* expertly weaves a poignant, old-fashioned story of love that begins on the wonderous and wild island where Charlotte is living the quiet and uneventful life of a wife and mom until the week her husband and son depart for a long fishing trip and the beautiful sailboat Shearwater delivers the handsome and mysterious Michael into Charlotte's life. Charlotte's carefully crafted equanimity is shattered and replaced with a once in a lifetime passion. As the storm appears and gathers strength, the romance intensifies with every turn of page until the surprising and satisfying ending."

JJ Flowers, Author of *Juan Pablo and the Butterflies*, a Westchester Fiction Award winner

"*Shearwater Storm* takes us to a remote island in the Pacific Northwest, where we meet a man wounded by an accident on his sailboat, Shearwater, and a woman alone while her husband and son are away. Unsettling circumstances bring these two together in Winer's riveting prose, when they are forced within a few days of knowing each other to reconcile their World War II experiences, mirrored in the desires of their present turmoil. *Shearwater Storm* is a multi-layered account of a hurricane force storm, and a storm within the heart, of making choices that might not be the right ones. Winer, an experienced nautical sailor, takes us on this remarkable journey to that deeper question. Once I started this novel, I could not put it down."

Kip Robinson Greenthal, Author of *Shoal Water*, winner of the Landmark Prize for Fiction and the Silver Medal Nautilus Book Award

"*Shearwater Storm* is a tale of self-discovery and love, an ode to the lush scenery of the Pacific Northwest while illustrating how we must at some point in our lives face the choices we've made in response to the inevitable sorrows of life."

Alicia Elkort, Author of *A Map of Every Undoing*

SHEARWATER STORM

Arthur Winer

Shearwater Storm
First edition, published 2023

By Arthur Winer

Cover Design by Arthur Winer with support from
Midjourney.com and Reprospace.com

Author Photo taken by Doug Marshall

Paperback ISBN-13: 978-1-952685-70-5

Published by Kitsap Publishing
Poulsbo, WA 98370
www.KitsapPublishing.com

For Judy

My Eternal Love

Shearwaters

—Soaring seabirds whose wings appear to "shear" wavetops, and who fly thousands of miles across the ocean without touching down on land.

Charlotte

As she pens today's date in her diary—April 21, 1958—Charlotte Rose counts twelve years that have passed since she fled California for a remote island of sea and sky and mountain. She sits at her oak desk, in what she calls her catch-all room at the back of the house, and wonders where these dozen years have gone. What they've brought her. And at what cost.

For more than a decade, the entries in her diary have focused on the joys and challenges of raising her son, Tommy. Now that he's older, he's pulling away from her—moving more toward his father—and this creates a nagging worry about what her future holds. Perhaps if she scribbles her concerns on the yellowing and brittle pages of her journal, seeing her fears in writing might lessen her anxiety.

But just as she's ready to face the blank page and record these secrets of her heart, she hears the footsteps of someone coming down the hall. Quickly, she closes the strap on her diary and locks it with a tiny key. Then she slips the leather-bound volume into a desk drawer and locks that with a larger key.

Rising from her desk, she turns to the rows of shelves lining the wall behind her, laden with the supplies and tools she needs to be self-sufficient on this small island. She reaches to the highest shelf and hides both keys inside a pair of dirt-covered garden gloves, behind a large bag of plant food. She feels safe with this choice of hiding place since her husband, Ben, has no special interest in gardening. Except when the peas or asparagus or tomatoes she's raised appear on his plate, in meals she's prepared for him and Tommy.

The footsteps she heard belong to her son, who appears now in the doorway. Although he's not quite twelve, already he's as tall as she is, tousle-haired and lanky. Despite his interruption of her attempt at diary writing, she delights in the sight of him.

He gives her a sheepish look. "Dad says we're ready to leave."

She's struck again by the strength of love she feels for her son.

"Tell your father I'll meet him at the dock."

"Hurry, Mom," her son urges, before turning away and rushing down the hall.

Minutes later, she stands on the weathered dock at the foot of their property, hugging Tommy to her with one hand as he tries to pull away. Ben is already aboard the *Emerald Rose*, warming the engine, and the choking odor of diesel exhaust envelops her as she holds her son.

"It's time to go!" Tommy pleads.

Letting him slip from her arm, she hands him a canvas bag with sandwiches. "Have a good time," she yells as he runs down the dock. "But you be safe, Tommy Rose!" she shouts. "And listen to your father!"

"I will, Mom," he calls, boosting himself over the trawler's railing with one hand.

She follows him down the dock and sees that Ben is not coming off the boat to say goodbye. There was a time when he would come to her on the dock and give her a hug, or even a kiss. But after seven years of marriage, he'd stopped. The spark, that had never been a flame, had left their relationship. Now she throws a small wave, and, from the wheelhouse, he waves back.

Ben is expecting her to cast off the lines, so she goes aft and releases the stern line first, throwing it over the rail to Tommy. Then she walks the length of the trawler, casts the bow line onto the foredeck and watches as Ben expertly backs the *Emerald Rose* away from the dock, turning the bow toward Eagle Cove's narrow entrance. Her last sight of them is Tommy waving from the stern as the trawler disappears around the north bluff.

A stiff breeze clears away the diesel exhaust, and after the trawler's wake laps against the far shore, the water becomes flat again, glistening green against the sunlight. Charlotte stays for a moment longer, taking in deep breaths of clean, sea air. A dozen sanderlings on the beach rise suddenly in a whirl of flashing wings and white bellies as they fly off. She turns and walks up the path to their home, between lines of rhododendrons she planted six or seven years before, their delicate purple and red blossoms emerging now in late April. As she climbs the porch steps, she looks forward to ten days of well-deserved time for herself.

On the porch, she sits on the bench and trades her house shoes for hiking boots. She lifts the seat of the bench and removes the small shoulder pack she keeps there. Then crossing the meadow below the house, she walks fast toward the trail to Keller Peak.

At the trailhead, she pauses for a moment and pulls her long auburn hair into a ponytail. Then, finding her stride, she hikes through a shaded ravine where the trail grows steep and her calf and thigh muscles strain against the rapid pace she has set. For forty minutes she follows long switchbacks, climbing through ancient forests of moss-covered cedars and firs. With this gain in elevation, the familiar unshackling of her heart begins. The higher she climbs, the lighter she feels. Until, near the summit, she imagines even a whisper of a breeze could float her off the steep face of the mountain, into the clouds.

Here, on Keller Peak—in the realm of eagles and hawks—she's free. To dream of soaring with these long-winged raptors on the thermals, high above the island.

Near the summit, the trail in front of her narrows, and although she knows the way as well as she knows the freckles on her arms, she tenses. To her right, the ground plunges into a dizzying void, mists hanging in the mountain clefts below. She recalls her first few months after arriving on Cambria Island, all those years ago, when she resisted the urge to fling herself off this precipice.

She was still filled then with the grief that drove her north to the open skies of Montana, seeking any kind of solace from her fiancé's death in the final days of the war. But the biting cold of winter there, and even the name of the mountains below which she lived—the Bitterroots—reminded her too much of her own bitterness at losing her love, David, and seemed not only to mirror her sorrow but also to mock it.

So, she headed west to Seattle, then north to this remote island off the Washington coast, a few miles south of the Canadian border. Now, although she's traveled this path on Keller Peak countless times, she never tires of its beauty. The giant, silent trees arouse in her the same reverence she'd felt at age fifteen in the cathedrals of Lyon and Paris—when her father took her to see the country where *his* father had been born. Hiking in this ancient forest, she feels as close to God now as she did then.

Finally, after an hour of hard hiking, she stands on the summit, lets the pack slide from her shoulders onto a flat boulder, and inhales the fragrance of pine scent. With the weight of the pack removed, she feels as light as the air itself. Reaching up, she removes her hair band, allowing her hair to shake free, spilling around her shoulders and down her back.

She pulls a canteen from her pack and washes the trail dust from her mouth. A brisk wind whips her hair around her face and carries the scent of drying mud flats up the mountain. The day is clear, and, from where she stands, all of Cambria Island lies below her—a rough oval, covered in dense primal forest, indented around its perimeter by rocky beaches and shallow blue inlets. At the south end of the island, Eagle Cove shimmers in the sunlight like a polished silver dollar. She can see her house and Ben's shop, tiny rectangles next to the green meadow that stretches down to the water. How many women, she wonders, can survey an entire island knowing they share it with fewer than three dozen other inhabitants?

Standing on Keller Peak's summit, she scans the vistas around her once more. She can see the *Emerald Rose*, a brown bug on the water, already pulling away from the island, making steady progress north. Silently, she wishes Ben and Tommy a rewarding father-son trip.

She sees only one other boat, in the far distance, and it's coming south from the Strait of Georgia. Something about it makes her think of a sailboat, although instead of white sails, the boat appears like a red dot on the blue sea. This puzzles her only for a moment. She turns away and walks over to her pack, lifts it easily onto her shoulders and heads down the path.

As she comes down the trail, she thinks of all the things she can accomplish for herself, now that she doesn't have to minister to the needs of her two men. Her garden will come first of course, but maybe she'll finally break out her brushes and oils and paint something. It would be the first time in many years she'd put pigments on a canvas. Despite all the promises she'd made to herself to resume painting, somehow, she hasn't found the right inspiration.

Michael

The sea is a dangerous lover.

She draws you out onto restless waters with her infinite beauty and unfathomable mysteries.

But if you relax into her seductive call, she will expose any weakness, any lack of humility you may have when you venture out onto her vast expanse.

If there are any truths Michael Cordero has learned in all his decades of sailing it is these. He's reminded of them now as he stands at the wheel of *Shearwater*, his forty-foot ketch, and surveys the seas surrounding him. Above him, a huge red spinnaker bellies out from the masthead, pulling the ketch against an ebbing tide that runs hard through the channel. He gives the wheel a half turn, and the boat slices through the foaming waves, spray pluming from its bow.

Raising his gaze from the straining spinnaker, he sees an eagle above, its breast open to the wind, executing a ballet on invisible thermals. He imagines what the eagle sees from its high vantage: green islands that appear to float on a blue sea; a man and his dog—tiny figures on a lone sailboat. Just this morning, he had raised anchor in a deep inlet where waterfalls cascaded in veils of mist and spray from high granite faces before plunging into the sea. Could the eagle, he wonders, be conscious of the incredible beauty of this place?

As the wind increases and the seas become more boisterous, he decides to douse the spinnaker. But at that moment Orion, his Siberian Husky, rises from the cockpit floor, ready to play. Michael crouches down, trying to keep the steering pedestal between himself and the dog. But Orion is too quick, and when the eager Siberian lunges at him in mock attack, Michael falls backwards under the Husky's formidable weight.

He smashes against the cockpit locker where the razor-sharp hook of his fishing gaff slices deep into the flesh below his left shoulder. When the pain hits, he feels a flash of irritation at Orion, but he won't raise his voice against his long-time sailing companion. Instead, he commands, "Orion, down," and the dog backs away.

As Michael struggles to his feet, he feels the gaff tear away from the wound under the weight of its long steel handle, hears it clatter behind him on the cockpit floor and, turning, sees the blood-stained hook glinting in the sun. He suppresses the urge to hurl the gaff into the sea when suddenly the water astern of the ketch boils in a cauldron of foam and spume and races towards *Shearwater* with frightening speed. Ignoring the shooting pain in his shoulder, he leaps for the mainsheet—after a lifetime of sailing, he recognizes the violence of this angry line squall.

"Orion, watch out!"

Before he can release the mainsheet, a ferocious wall of wind slams *Shearwater* on her side, forces the sails down to the roiling water, and flings the two of them against the lifelines.

As the ketch struggles to right herself, Michael claws his way up the slanted cockpit, flinching from the ache of his wound. He un-cleats the mainsheet, and the line burns through his fingers. The boom swings out until the mainsail flogs in a deafening clatter of whipping Dacron and vibrating metal. He reaches to release the line to the spinnaker, but the huge red sail explodes with a sound like a gunshot.

"Damnit to hell!" he roars into the maelstrom, his left shoulder screaming now. For several minutes, he can only cling to the wheel with his good hand as the ketch flees across the Strait on a hissing wake. Then, with the same abruptness as its arrival, the squall passes —leaving ranks of steep whitecaps marching across the water.

Michael sags with relief and confirms that Orion is safe in the cockpit. Locking the wheel, he retrieves his medical kit from the cabin. With his left arm already hanging useless at his side, he strips off the blood-soaked layers of his clothes, wondering how deep the hook had gone in. Bare-chested and shivering, he tries to place a bandage over the slash in his back. But no matter which way he stretches his right arm, he can't reach the seeping wound. After several minutes he gives up.

"I'll have to rig something," he mutters to himself. With his teeth and right hand, he enlarges a hole in his worn T-shirt and manages to rip it along its length. Then he rolls the torn shirt into an elongated pad and loops it around his back, over the wound. He ties the ends of the T-shirt over his chest and struggles into his camouflage shirt and sailing jacket. He glances at Orion, lying on the cockpit floor curled into himself, and is again reassured the Husky is okay.

Standing at the wheel, Michael does a three-sixty scan with binoculars, but there are no other vessels in sight. If his VHF radio worked, he could send a distress message, and somewhere in the area a vessel might respond, but the radio stopped working in Fitz Hugh Sound.

He knows he needs help, and soon, but feels no panic. He's faced enough emergencies while sailing, has been alone on the sea for so many passages across oceans that he's learned to control his emotions even in the most challenging conditions. Still, he curses his inattention to the fishing gaffe, so unlike his typical care of the boat.

He clutches the navigation chart with his good hand and scans the nearby waters. It's not obvious where he can find immediate help. Anacortes or Bellingham are at least two hours away even if he runs the diesel wide open. The closest island is Cambria, barely a speck on the chart, with a small bay guarded by a reef at its shallow entrance. Running his finger over the charted depths, he sees that *Shearwater's* deep keel can pass through that entrance only at the highest tides. Quickly, he thumbs the worn pages of the tide table until he comes to the proper entry. He sags when he sees the water surrounding Cambria Island has already started to ebb.

Orion's blue eyes follow him with curiosity. "Well, my friend," Michael says, "the seas are bigger now. Maybe we can ride a swell through that entrance." There's a huge risk of damaging the hull, he thinks, but he sees no other options.

With his good hand, he tacks *Shearwater's* bow through the wind and adjusts the mainsheet. Even this small effort brings waves of dizziness and spasms of pain across his back. He suspects he might be suffering from hypothermia, and after a long day on the water and the blood he's lost, his injured body craves sleep. But he knows that if he allows himself to slip into unconsciousness and the bleeding were to continue, he might never wake. He imagines *Shearwater* drifting at sea with Orion stranded and starving. He won't allow that.

As the ketch approaches Cambria Island, Michael turns on the depth-sounder and watches the bottom come up fast. In the lee of the mountainous island the wind dies, and the *Shearwater* begins to slow.

He hits the starter button. When the sailboat's diesel engine cranks over, he shoves the throttle forward, his left shoulder cramping with each movement. He grabs a lifeline as a wave of blackness passes behind his eyes.

As he regains his balance, a narrow opening appears in the island's granite face revealing a small cove. He lifts the binoculars and sees among the alders and maples on the far side of the cove, a weathered two-story house, its windows staring like eyes across the water. But it's the thin plume of smoke curling from the chimney that holds his attention.

He slams the wheel hard to starboard and heads for the narrow entrance. When the alarm on the depth-sounder begins to shriek, his heart jumps. "I'm not sure we'll make this, Orion!" The Husky raises his muzzle, his brown ears flicking up.

A hundred yards into the opening, the boat staggers, knocking Orion off his feet and flinging Michael against the steering pedestal.

For a moment, he thinks his ketch is hard aground. But when he shoves the throttle wide open, the diesel roars, and *Shearwater* shoots forward, gliding into the cove.

Charlotte

The rough-skinned potato, sprouting tiny root hairs, slips from Charlotte 's hands as she stares out her kitchen window. A white-hulled sailboat, its bow and stern shaped in long graceful lines, has suddenly appeared in the narrow entrance to the cove below her home. She lifts the potato to the sink counter as the sleek vessel drifts towards the center of her small bay like a white ghost ship. Dozens of gulls fly up from the gleaming surface of the sea, their wings flared to the wind as they wheel and dip in great arcs around the slowing boat. Through the half-opened window, she hears their raucous cries.

"I'll be damned," she says out loud. "I didn't think a sailboat could get in here."

She knows the entrance reef is too shallow for the deep keels of sailboats. Only luck or great skill could bring a deep-drafted vessel to the foot of her land. Standing in her kitchen, she flashes back to her childhood, when her father bought a dilapidated gaff-rigged sloop with money he'd made in the stock market, and they both learned to sail the boat together. To that point in her young life, she'd never felt so alive as she had the afternoon she and her dad sailed out on San Francisco Bay for the first time, a strong breeze blowing in her hair, the boat slicing through waves, one of the happiest days of her childhood.

Now, still not taking her gaze from the window, she dries her hands as this intruding sailboat comes to rest a mere thirty yards off the pebble beach below her house. She watches as a man walks forward to the bow, a big silver and black Husky at his heels. Although he moves with an agility that speaks of years on the decks of boats, the man favors his left arm, and his restrained movements suggest he's in pain. He drops the anchor off the bow, returns to the stern and pulls in the inflatable dinghy trailing behind the sailboat. With one hand he lowers himself into the small tender, and his dog leaps off the sailboat into the dinghy's stern.

Realizing this stranger intends to come to her dock and climb the path leading to the front porch, she hurries to her catch-all room, and, in a worn leather case, finds the birder's binoculars she uses to study the herons and snowy egrets that like to forage in the tidal flats on the north side of the cove.

Back in the kitchen, she trains the binoculars on the figure in the inflatable dinghy. The man is big-shouldered and long-limbed, with an angular face and a thatch of unruly dark hair. Using only one oar at the stern, he sculls the small boat toward her dock. She can count on the fingers of one hand the number of times a stranger has come to her house over the past ten years, and in every case Ben and Tommy have been with her.

Opening the hall closet, she lifts a twelve-gauge shotgun from its case and breaks open both barrels to confirm the cartridges are in place. All her life, she's hated guns. But early in their marriage, Ben bought her this shotgun and insisted she keep it in the house. "While I'm gone fishing, you and Tommy are here by yourselves," he argued. "Suppose a black bear swims over from another island? Or the wrong kind of stranger shows up?" She had no answer to that. "The beauty of a shotgun," he told her, "is that you don't have to aim it much to stop something."

Now she feels grateful Ben persuaded her to keep the weapon clean and ready. Carrying the shotgun into the living room, she stands behind the curtains in the front window and watches as the tall stranger and his dog climb onto her dock. As he approaches her house, she sees a dark stain, blood perhaps, running down one leg of his jeans.

Hardly breathing, she waits to see what he does next.

Michael

He feels so weak after he pulls himself onto the dock's weathered planks that he needs to rest on one knee. When he manages to stand, his vision swims. To keep from falling, he grabs a dock piling and steadies himself.

Orion follows him across the dock ramp and up the path to the house. At the porch steps, he stops to rest again. Grimacing, he leans on the handrail and drags his feet up the four wooden stairs, aware of the odor of wood smoke and the possibility of help. Telling Orion to sit, he bangs on the screen door.

No one answers.

He tries to catch his breath, causing a sharp stab in his shoulder, and pounds on the door again, louder this time.

Still no answer.

He bangs once more, his strength ebbing.

Silence.

"Please, I'm injured!"

His own words sound distant, as if shouted by someone else across the cove.

He's about to try the back of the house when the front door cracks open. A woman stands half-visible behind the screen door with hair falling in copper rivulets to her waist. He takes a step closer and sees a mixture of alarm and curiosity in her eyes.

"My name is Michael Cordero," he tells her, gesturing toward his ketch. "I'm off the S*hearwater.*" When she makes no response, he adds, "I have a fishing gaff wound in my back that I can't treat myself. Can you help me?"

A look of wariness passes across the woman's face, and he realizes she might be afraid of him. Hoping to reassure her, he steps back from the door and a sudden wave of nausea and dizziness overtakes him. His knees buckle and he falls backwards.

He tries to catch himself as Orion jumps aside, but his head strikes a glancing blow against the porch railing and Orion's whimper is the last thing he hears before a merciful darkness swallows him.

Charlotte

As the man falls, she has a powerful urge to close and lock the door. Instead, she lunges to catch him. *Too late*. He's down by the time she's on the porch, the Siberian Husky hovering over him. Now she can see the man's shirt is soaked with blood.

She crouches next to the dog with her left hand extended. The Siberian locks his blue eyes on her, and she offers the scent on her hands before reaching to touch his head and rub his ears. Then she bends to the man, places a finger on his neck and finds a decent pulse.

She props up the man's head with a cushion from a porch chair and races into the catch-all room, trying to remember the first aid she'll need. Much of what she knows comes from medical guidebooks she relies on to treat any small injuries or illnesses she and Ben or Tommy have living on this remote island. She has the necessary medical supplies and after dumping the laundry out of its basket, she loads tape, antiseptic, a bottle of rubbing alcohol, butterfly bandages and rolls of gauze, then grabs a sleeping bag off a nearby shelf.

On the porch, the Husky whines and circles the man and tries to lick his face. Gently elbowing the dog aside, she kneels to her work, ignoring her queasiness.

She heaves the man into an upright position and works off his yellow slicker, then attempts to unbutton his camouflage shirt. For a moment, his head straightens, and he looks at her with glassy eyes before his head rolls over again.

Feeling the urgency, she pulls off his shirt and shivers at the sight of his bloodied bare skin, his muscled shoulders, and arms. She hesitates for an instant. *What if he bleeds to death, here on my porch?*

She removes the makeshift T-shirt bandage, wet with blood, and opens the bottle of rubbing alcohol. Working quickly, she cleans the wound, then the skin around the wound, her hands moving in front of her as if they are attached to someone else's arms. His injury doesn't seem as serious as she first feared, and, after she pulls the two edges of skin together, she seals them with butterfly bandages and then tapes a thick gauze pad over the slash with three long adhesives. Then she wraps his torso and the gauze pads with white bandaging to keep pressure on the sealed wound.

With care, she lays him on his right side and washes the dried blood from his hands. His palms are broad, his fingers long, with trim nails. She notices he doesn't wear a ring, but there's calluses on his palms and what looks to be rope burns. Still, his hands and fingers are smoother than Ben's, which are always nicked and torn from working with hooks, nets, and wire ropes.

With warm water, she cleans the man's back, feeling his skin taut over muscle, then cradles his head in her lap to clean his face and neck. His expression is peaceful, as though he's sleeping. His mouth is broad, his closed eyes wideset, and she notices the fullness of his lips. His thick hair is disheveled but soft to the touch.

While she dries him with a clean bath towel, she studies him in the day's waning light. She's known the bodies of only two men—her beloved David, lost to the war in his youth, and Ben, who's gained weight in recent years—and she feels an illicit pleasure looking at this man without his knowledge. His torso is firm, his belly flat, not like the island fishermen with their beer-drinking and fatty foods. She knows just enough from sailing with her father to understand that constantly raising and lowering sails, grinding winches, and balancing against the endless motion of the boat makes every muscle work. As a result, this Michael Cordero—she thinks she heard him say this name—is lean and solid.

When she probes beneath the hair at the back of his head, she finds a small swelling but no break in the skin, and she assumes this is where he hit his head when he fell against the porch railing. She puts a forefinger to his wrist: his pulse feels stronger now. Pulling back his eyelids, she sees that his pupils are neither dilated nor constricted, a good sign. When she puts the back of her hand to his forehead, she finds no fever. How urgently does he need professional attention, she wonders? Should she call over to Richardson Island and the nearest doctor? *Save that until you've done the best you can for him*, she tells herself. Who knows how long it will take a doctor to come over anyway, especially with the line squalls that have plagued the island in the last few days.

She opens the sleeping bag she brought to the porch, lays it out next to him and rolls him onto half of it. Then she pulls the other half of the bag over his body and zips it closed. She props the screen door open with one of the wicker chairs, grabs the top of the sleeping bag and straining against his dead weight, pulls the bag a few inches at a time through the doorway into the living room. Breathing in ragged gasps, she stands over him, her heart beating hard.

The Husky has followed them into the room, and she worries about her cat. She tries to pull the dog back onto the porch, but he eludes her grasp and returns to the man's prone form. *Give it up, Charlotte, Toby will know where to hide.*

She places a pillow from the couch under the man's head, then kneads the sore muscles in her neck and shoulders. Before closing the front door, she sees the dark forms of rabbits—cottontails—darting on the meadow in the blue light of dusk. As the night comes on, the living room grows colder, and she places three logs in the wood stove and stirs the red embers from the fire she built this morning.

In the kitchen, she scrubs the blood from her hands and arms. Standing at the sink, she drinks a glass of water and glances at the sailboat lying at anchor, a graceful white form in the fading light. She wonders what kind of man this vessel brought to her home.

After she carries his bloodied clothes and her towels to the laundry room, she slices pieces of cooked and boned chicken onto a plate for his dog and then fills a water bowl. The Husky pads over to her, and she rubs his head, stroking his white muzzle. He licks her hand, then tries to lick her face before turning to the chicken pieces. His dog appears to be intelligent and well cared for. Whatever else might be true of the man lying on her living room floor, he has good taste in dogs and is clearly kind to his Husky. Rational or not, because of this, she feels a little more comfortable with this stranger being in her house.

At the dining table, she picks at a bit of the chicken and the vegetables left from the previous night. But after a few bites her stomach churns with apprehension. She pushes the plate away. What if he wakes and becomes irrational or violent?

In the living room, she checks his jeans pockets. No wallet. No credit cards. No identification or personal effects. Just a braided cord—probably to tie something on his boat—and one of those all-purpose Swiss army knives, an oily chamois rag, and two threaded bolts. Not exactly a complete biography. He doesn't need to carry money or identification while sailing, she realizes, any more than she does, living on this tiny island. He can keep those things in a safe place on his boat.

She considers motoring her skiff out to his sailboat and searching his vessel. She might piece together some sense of who he is. But she's too exhausted and unsettled. Instead, after confirming he's still sleeping, she carries the shotgun upstairs and lays it on the floor next to the bed and then turns the lock Ben installed on the bedroom door when Tommy was four, so he wouldn't walk in on them.

Soaking in a hot bath, she scrubs her hair and skin until all traces of the man's blood are gone. With a worn nail file, she scrapes the dried blood from under her fingernails, and when she gets to the fourth finger on her left hand, she stares at the polished silver band and its intricate Haida carvings. This was the ring she told Ben she wanted a dozen years ago, when he asked her to be his wife, the day he stood downstairs, even more shy than usual—as though fearing she might still refuse him—his face flushed above his full beard, one hand fidgeting with a button on his shirt.

Rising from the tub, she still can't articulate all the reasons she had agreed to marry him, although she knows passion wasn't one of them. It had been more about Ben's generous and decent nature, his eagerness to help her when she first arrived on the island, and his acceptance of her need to be alone in those early months of grieving. When the time came to decide about marrying him, it was her desire to have a child and her acceptance that she would never find another love like the one she'd had with David. A woman gets only one chance for a soulmate in a lifetime, she'd told herself.

After toweling herself dry, she pulls on a nightgown. She finds Toby, her Siamese, wedged into the furthest corner behind the bed, brown paws tucked under his cream-colored body. "It's okay, Toby," she whispers. "We'll have our house back soon." She offers his food and water bowls that she had earlier brought upstairs and sits cross-legged on the floor while she strokes his soft coat.

Then she climbs into bed and, despite her apprehension, sleep comes quickly.

Michael

It's not sound, he decides, that draws him up from a deep sleep. The house is quiet: no clocks ticking, no radio or television blaring, not even murmuring from the next room. He recalls landing on the island and approaching the woman behind the screen door but little else. Now, in the sleeping bag covering him, he feels bandages taped on his back and wonders if it was the woman at the door who treated him.

Orion is not in the living room, and this concerns him. Right now, the big Husky feels like the only one he can rely on, and Michael wishes his loyal dog was at his side.

Raising his head, he sees a ragged couch hugging one wall, its flower-print fabric worn and faded, a lamp table at both ends. An easy chair sits on the opposite side of the room. He can see a large painting covering almost the entire wall above the couch—broad swirls of raging color: ochre, vermilion, black, various shades of purple. He's drawn to this painting, the energy behind it, emotions he can only guess embedded in it. But the painting also makes him uneasy, the same uneasiness he'd felt at the Van Gogh Museum in Amsterdam, viewing the dark, brooding paintings Van Gogh had made early in his career. This was one of many museums he'd visited during his time in Europe, before the Spanish Civil war broke out. Now, he wonders who created this painting of such extraordinary, dark beauty.

When he hears Orion bark outside, he pushes off the sleeping bag and struggles to his feet, swaying on unsteady legs. He tests his left shoulder, finds the pain bearable and then glances around the room for his shirt and sailing jacket but doesn't see them. Orion barks again. Now, he sees someone has left a large pitcher of water and a glass on the side table for him. He drinks two full glasses of water and part of a third before satisfying his powerful thirst.

He moves out onto the porch and sees *Shearwater* swinging to her anchor against a gentle breeze. Reflected madrona trees and a slice of blue sky shimmer on the water, and sparrows twitter in blackberry vines that run wild along one side of the house. A blue heron lifts from the edge of the water, spreads its broad wings and, legs trailing, flies a hundred yards down the gravel beach before settling again in a tidal pool. The scene from this porch is idyllic, like a morning at sea.

He takes in this pastoral view and then sees the woman digging in a flowerbed near the house. The intensity of her concentration on the daffodils and tulips in front of her, moves something inside him—a longing for companionship, for a woman's voice. He's been alone with Orion at sea for so long now, and all that time the opportunity to enjoy the company of a woman has eluded him.

Charlotte

On all fours at the front of the house, she's cutting flowers and pulling weeds when the injured man appears on her front porch, silent as an apparition. That he stands there at all, after the condition she found him in yesterday afternoon, amazes her. Earlier, when she'd come downstairs and found him sleeping, she'd assumed he might sleep for most of the morning but left water for him in case he awoke.

But now he's on her front porch, naked from the waist up, only the white bandaging around his torso where she'd placed it last night. Startled at the sight of him, she wipes sweat from her forehead with the back of a gloved hand. She becomes aware her V-necked shirt has fallen away from her chest, exposing her bra to his vantage on the porch. But his gaze never leaves her face, his eyes searching hers in a way that makes her even more aware of her body. Still, a hint of something soulful in him causes her to hold his gaze.

Setting down her trowel and pulling off her gloves, she rises, dusts off the knees of her jeans and approaches the porch, now sensing shyness in his broad face. He's taller than she realized while he was lying prone on her porch. She considers herself tall, but he stands a full head higher, with big shoulders and that shock of dark hair.

As she climbs the porch steps, she tries to shake off a growing sense of complicity in the arrival of this handsome man and his dog. *I've done nothing to lure him here*, she tells herself.

The seconds tick away as he stands calmly waiting on the porch.

She's struck by his ease, despite his wound. "How are you feeling?" she calls to him.

"Better," he says smiling. "Much better."

"You gave me a scare yesterday."

"You took care of me?"

She nods.

"I'm so grateful," he says. "I know I must have frightened you. I didn't have any other options."

"We're a long way from anything. Out here on this rock."

"That's what my charts showed."

"Your name is Michael Cordero?" she asks, climbing the porch steps. "That's what I heard, just before you fell and hit your head."

"Is that why I have a headache?" he asks, putting a hand on the bump at the back of his head. "I can't remember anything after I made it to your front door."

"You were out cold. But you had a strong pulse. And your eyes looked normal, so I didn't call for help. My name is Charlotte Rose," she says, extending her hand.

"This is some way to meet," he says, shaking her hand. "But I'm grateful to know you, Charlotte Rose."

She notes his strong handshake, and again a hint of shyness in his eyes.

"Apologies for being like this," he says, releasing her hand and gesturing to his bare torso. "I couldn't find my shirt, and I'm wondering if you've seen my dog."

"Your shirt is hanging on the clothesline back of the house," she tells him. "And your Husky is fine. He stayed with you most of the night. But after I fed him this morning, I put him in a run we have at the back of the shop, so you could keep sleeping."

"I'm in your debt," he says, his voice resonant with appreciation.

She shrugs, embarrassed by his gratitude. Ben and Tommy rarely thank her for anything.

"I'll get your shirt, and your dog."

He smiles and offers a simple, "Thank you."

She notes the sincerity in his voice. Not just polite formality. And she detects an accent in his speech. From somewhere in New England, she guesses. His 'a's are drawn out. If he said car, she thinks it would sound more like *cah*. But he has only a trace of this accent. As if he's lost most of it by being away from its source for a long time.

"I'll be going back to my boat," he assures her. "I won't be troubling you further."

An impulse springs from a place inside her she hasn't visited in a long time—a feeling that she doesn't want him to leave, at least not yet.

"I should look at your wound," she tells him. "You might need a clean dressing."

He hesitates, but then says, "You're right. I can't do that myself."

"Come back inside," she says, motioning to the front door.

The laundry basket with the first aid supplies is where she left it next to the fireplace. She brings it over to the dining table and reaches for a chair.

"I can do that," he says. With his good arm, he turns the chair around and straddles it facing away from her. She senses the same shyness in him she detected earlier, and as she stands behind him, she's conscious of his scent, warm and masculine.

Carefully, she removes the bandages and examines the wound. "Just a bit of oozing between the butterfly bandages," she tells him. "I'll clean the area with rubbing alcohol and put on a fresh bandage. The alcohol might sting a bit."

He laughs. "Nothing like the pain yesterday, when that gaff went into me."

Soaking a paper towel with rubbing alcohol, she cleans the area and applies a new bandage, conscious of touching his skin with her fingers, of the individual vertebrae in his back, her proximity to him and the intimacy of it all. "I think you're good for a while now," she says, coming around to face him. "As long as you don't strain that shoulder too much. I'll get your dog and your clothes now. What's your dog's name?"

"His name is Orion. I'll wait on the porch," he says, rising and replacing the chair under the dining table.

He looks right at her. In an instant all the routine, daily rituals of her life, the mundane and commonplace aspects of it, seem upended. Staring into his eyes she feels a dormant curiosity awaken. She wants to know more about Michael Cordero, this man who has sailed into her life without warning, from who knows where.

Michael

Outside, he watches as she moves down the porch with the long easy strides of a practiced hiker. Her work clothes and long hair don't do much to hide her figure, and he's not sorry about that. He wonders about her, what she's doing here, living on such an isolated island. One so small and out of the way he's never paid attention to it on previous sails down the Inside Passage. He thinks there might be more to this woman than her garden, and the flowers and vegetables she's raising, and he wonders if perhaps she made the striking painting in her living room.

Out on the water, gulls squabble over a floating object of some kind. A cloud passes in front of the sun and the air feels cool on his bare torso. He sits in one of the cushioned wicker chairs, content to watch his sailboat bob at anchor in the cove. After the cloud drifts off, sunlight falls on the water's surface, shimmering.

The seagulls cease their squawking now, and, after a few minutes, the woman comes around the corner of the house carrying his camouflage shirt in one hand and his yellow foul weather jacket under her arm. Orion is behind her and comes bounding up to him.

"Missed, you, buddy," he says, leaning down to rub the Husky's head and flanks.

When he straightens up, she hands him his clothes, a palpable shyness rising between them.

Now that they're in better light and standing close, he sees she spends a lot of time in the sun: chapped lips and the first hints of sunspots amid her freckles, squint lines at the corners of her eyes. He guesses she's a few years younger than he is, maybe in her late thirties. She wears no makeup or jewelry, only her hair brushed to a sheen giving evidence of attention to appearance. But for him there is something beautiful about this woman, more than the long waves of auburn hair and piercing dark jade eyes, something indefinable but striking.

As she stands framed in sunlight, he tries to imagine her life on this island and cannot, even for a moment, glimpse it. With his good hand, he pulls his shirt over his bandaged back. He senses her studying him. As if he's an exotic animal. Or perhaps she sees him as an invasive species, washed up on her beach on an incoming tide.

Charlotte

They stand on the porch, awkwardly facing each other.

"You're from the east coast," she says. "You have a slight accent."

"I thought I'd lost it," he says, with a half-smile. "I grew up in Narragansett Bay. And I spent four years in Maine building my boat. Their accent is so pronounced, I think I picked up some of it."

For the second time this morning, she has an impulse to invite him to stay longer, to learn more about him.

"Can you eat something?" She tries to say this casually but feels as if she's holding her breath, waiting for his answer.

He shrugs. "You've done so much already."

"We're ready for emergencies out here," she says, explaining away the help she gave him.

"You and your husband?" he asks, gesturing to the Haida ring on her left hand.

"And my son Tommy." She thinks about telling him that they're both away fishing, but she doesn't know him. Although, she has an instinct about Michael Cordero already, that she has nothing to fear from him. But it's only an instinct, something his eyes and demeanor have been telling her during their conversation, along with his wanting to return to his boat.

She studies him. His face is open now, nothing guarded there.

"Anyone on this island would've done the same," she says. "An unwritten code. We rely on each other for help when we really need it."

"I can see why that would be important," he says, "on a small island like this one."

"Look, I'm going to fix breakfast for myself," she says. "It's just as easy to cook for two. And you need to make up for all that lost blood."

"If you're fixing something for yourself," he says, "I'm grateful to join you."

"Good," she replies, pulling open the screen door. "You can wait in the dining room while I wash off this garden grime."

Michael

He follows her through the front door to the dining room table and pulls out a chair while she disappears down the hall. Glancing around the room, he sees it hasn't been painted in a while, and years of fireplace use in the house have left a woodsmoke odor. But there's a vase on the dining table filled with yellow and red tulips that brighten the room.

"This won't take long," she says, coming into the kitchen and beginning breakfast preparations.

From where he sits, he can see an old stove and a small refrigerator that stands against the far wall, opposite a sink flanked by a set of worn cupboards. Colored drawings of animals and sea creatures are taped to the refrigerator door, made by her son, Tommy, he concludes. Below the drawings are photos of a man and a boy that he assumes are her husband and son, at what looks like a county fair, a small Ferris wheel and other amusement rides in the background.

The kitchen reminds him of his mother's kitchen, in the first house his parents owned in Newport, Rhode Island—the one they lived in while his father started a career as a naval architect and later fought in the trenches in France during the World War. Charlotte Rose's kitchen has the same well-used coziness, the same feeling of a woman's ownership: metal canisters arrayed from large-to-small on the counter; embroidered dish towels hanging from a ring next to the sink; a faded-yellow drain board under the plastic dish rack.

Her house transports him back to his early years, growing up as something of a loner at school, awkward with girls, even though they seemed to like him. And first learning to sail on Narragansett Bay in a small boat his father originally designed for a client. His over-riding memory of his mother from those days was of her towering strength, her determination to hold her family together with love and caring no matter what problems arose, especially after his father returned to her from that brutal war mostly silent and brooding, with problems sleeping and controlling his temper.

"Do you like coffee or tea?" Charlotte asks him.

He thinks for a moment. "If you have herbal tea," he tells her, "I would take that. I'm planning to rest when I get back to the boat."

Charlotte

She puts the kettle on to boil and selects half a dozen chanterelle mushrooms from her dwindling collection. Rummaging in the utensil drawer, she finds one of the few knives she keeps sharpened. She feels his eyes on her, but for some reason his gaze doesn't make her uncomfortable, not like the looks some of the men on the island give her.

Slicing the mushrooms into thin wafers, she dices two large tomatoes. Then she lights the burner under a large iron skillet, adds butter, and slides the mushrooms and tomatoes off the cutting board into the pan.

"You can sleep in the middle of the day on your boat?" she asks him while she breaks four eggs into a large bowl and beats them with a whisk.

"Most of the time," he answers. "It's not often you get a full night's sleep at sea sailing solo, especially in a big sea state. Or in variable winds. You get used to cat-napping between sail changes, whenever you can."

She tries to imagine what it would be like sailing by herself on the ocean, far from land, and decides it would take a special kind of person to find contentment doing that. The kind of person sitting at her dining room table apparently, studying her as she pours the eggs into the skillet, over the sauteed mushrooms and tomatoes. She lets the eggs firm while she cuts thick slices of the whole grain bread she baked the day before and slides them into the toaster. In the silverware drawer, she finds a knife that's not too dull and a fork with only one bent tine. She pumps fresh water into a plastic cup and sets the water and the utensils in front of Michael Cordero, feeling a bit like a diner waitress.

Even after years of making breakfast for Tommy and Ben, it feels like a small miracle when everything comes together at the same time. She slides two-thirds of the browned omelet onto a plate, adds the toast, pours hot water over chamomile leaves in a large tea pot, and places it all in front of him, with a large pewter mug. Then she serves herself.

Somehow it all seems normal, sitting across her dining table from a total stranger, sharing breakfast with him, while Ben and Tommy are up north, fishing for salmon.

Michael

They eat in silence for a few minutes before he tells her, "This is all delicious."

"I'm glad you're enjoying it," she responds.

He notices she's barely touching her omelet and didn't make toast for herself. But she does drink the tea, cradling the mug as steam rises. He sees intelligence in her eyes.

She says, "On the porch yesterday, and again this morning, you mentioned something about a fishing gaff."

He rests his fork on his plate. "That's how I was wounded. Do you know what a fishing gaff is?"

Her eyes flicker for an instant. "My husband is a commercial fisherman."

He feels heat come into his face. "Sorry, I should have guessed you'd know all about fishing out here."

She makes no indication of being offended and asks, "How did the accident happen?"

Relieved, he says, "I pulled in a salmon at Galliano Island and neglected to put the gaffe away afterwards. Orion likes to play a game with me around the steering pedestal and usually I'm quick enough to dodge him. But not this time."

She sips the steaming tea. "I was surprised to see a sailboat come in here."

"When I saw the smoke from your chimney, I decided to try for it, even though *Shearwater* draws six feet," he says. "Given the tide yesterday, I don't know how we cleared the reef at your entrance. But I'm grateful for it. Not sure how it would have ended if you hadn't helped me."

She motions toward his plate. "I didn't mean to keep you from finishing."

He resumes eating, and when he's done with his eggs, he asks, "Will you have that last piece of toast?"

She slides the toast plate over to him. "You weren't in any shape for dinner last night. You must be starved."

"I did wake up famished," he says, smiling, "but I'm good now."

While he butters the toast, she says, "I noticed you wear a camouflage shirt. Were you in the war?"

His chest tightens. "Navy," he answers, slowly. "PT boats… in the Pacific."

He doesn't add that he served in the same naval squadron as John F. Kennedy. Or that his PT boat was sliced in half by the same enemy destroyer that sank Kennedy's boat that night in the Solomon Islands. It might seem to her he was trading on Kennedy's growing fame, especially now that JFK appeared to be running for President—that he was trying to impress her. But he has a deeper reason for not wanting to tell her any of this, something he's never revealed to anyone from that night in August 1943.

"Is that how you got into sailing?" she asks, genuine curiosity on her face.

He shakes his head, finishing the toast. "Sailing started long before that for me, when I was a boy growing up in Rhode Island."

"So, you sail a lot?" she asks, setting her tea mug down.

"Full time."

"You don't have to work?" A hint of surprise in her voice.

"I sell sailing articles and stories to magazines."

"Have I seen any of them?"

"Do you read the magazines *Look* or *Life*?"

"I don't," she says, shaking her head.

"Well unless you read *Yachting* or *Sail,* I guess not."

"There's a cliche about starving writers," she says smiling. "But you make a living at it?"

"I do make money writing, but I also repair diesel engines. In places that have no diesel mechanics. I guess that's something you could call work," he says. "That and writing brings in enough to take care of *Shearwater*. And the basics for Orion and me. Our needs are simple."

"No family?" she asks. "No obligations?"

Her voice is skeptical again, and he feels self-conscious explaining himself this way. "None of that," he says.

Her questions are probing, and it's been a long time since someone has taken this much interest in him. But a darkness moves through him as he recalls the death of his wife. And with that lurking memory, one that is never far from his mind, he finds himself unable to continue the conversation.

He pushes back from the table and takes both their empty plates and silverware to the kitchen sink, then runs hot water over them. When he returns to the table, her surprise at this gesture is obvious on her face. But taking dishes to the kitchen after meals was one of the few things his mother ever asked of him. Out of habit he sometimes still does it. Mostly, his mother had let him spend every free day sailing out on Narragansett Bay while he yearned for the open sea.

"Thanks for a fine breakfast," he tells her. "Orion and I should go now. I need to rest. Then I must put the boat back together, after the knockdown we suffered in that squall."

Charlotte

Standing with Michael Cordero in her dining room, she surprises herself for the third time that morning. On a whim, she says, "You could rest on the couch, instead of going back to your boat."

Where are these impulses coming from, she wonders?

"The couch pulls out," she adds, gesturing toward the living room. "I can get a clean blanket." But the skeptical expression on his face tells her she should have let it go at making him breakfast.

He doesn't answer immediately. Then he says, "I've imposed on you enough."

"It's not been an imposition," she answers, knowing this is not at all how she felt last night, when she thought he might bleed to death on the porch. How would she have explained that to Ben?

But when she sees he won't change his mind, the concern she had last night that she might not be able to remove him from her house turns into a pang of disappointment that he's leaving.

"I can run you out in my skiff?" she stammers, trying to cover her miscalculation. "You wouldn't have to use your left arm rowing."

He shakes his head. "It's not that far, and I can scull with one oar with my good arm. You were brilliant at patching me together," he says with a warm smile. "You should apply for a medical license."

She laughs and follows him onto the porch.

"Come, Orion!" he says, and the Husky runs up from the meadow, his tail beating hard.

Michael Cordero turns and gives her a small salute with his right hand. "Thank you again," he says, his hazel eyes sincere. "You've been kind and generous. And you most likely saved my life."

"You're welcome," is all she can think to say, still flustered about offering him the couch.

Sagging into one of the wicker chairs, she watches him stride down the path, Orion trotting behind. At the dock, he lowers himself into his inflatable dinghy, and the Husky jumps in after him.

Out on the cove, the water is a shade of translucent blue, like glacial ice. A color an artist would use, she thinks, *a color I could use if I ever get to painting again*.

She sees Michael Cordero fit an oar into an oarlock on the transom of his dinghy and then scull toward the ketch. He's looking back at her now as he faces astern, and she feels self-conscious about watching him. Rising, she steps to the screen door and waves to him. He waves back, not a perfunctory flick of his wrist but a wide sweep of his right arm.

Inside the living room, she tries to remember all the things she promised herself she would accomplish once he was out of her house. The list she'd made last week, knowing Ben and Tommy would be away for almost two weeks, was a long one. But now her mind can't stop thinking about Michael Cordero and how he moved down her path with an animal-like grace.

***

For two days after he's returned to his boat, she glances from time to time towards the white-hulled ketch, straining to catch a glimpse of him, to see if he's all right. She wonders if he needs more care and even considers motoring out to his boat to check on him. But she doesn't know how private he might be. And folks on the water don't generally appreciate someone showing up at their boat uninvited.

Michael Cordero does appear early in the mornings. She sees him row Orion to the far end of the cove and then they disappear for a time into the orange-barked madronas and tall cedars, before he rows back to his boat. When, on the afternoon of the second day, she sees him sitting out in the cockpit in the sun, resting for several hours, she feels reassured he must be okay.

By the third morning she believes that any time now Michael Cordero will pull up anchor and sail out the entrance and she'll never see him again.

As the day wears on she tries to convince herself it won't matter to her if he sails away.

But that would be a lie.

Michael

On his third morning at anchor, Michael emerges from the main hatch refreshed after a night of sound sleep. Already his left shoulder feels better, and the wound is healing well. He owes this to Charlotte Rose, and he wonders how to thank her before he tries to force *Shearwater* back through Eagle Cove's entrance on the highest tide of the month, a week from now.

He removes two crab traps from the stern cockpit locker and loads them into the dinghy, then climbs in and tells Orion, "Stay, I'll be right back." He has no way of knowing if Eagle Cove has good crabbing, but he'll give it a try.Rowing to the far side of the cove, he pauses the inflatable in fifty feet of water. With the awl on his marine knife, he punctures six holes in a can of dog food and places the can inside the first trap. Then he swings the trap out over the water and drops it with a splash. He watches the yellow cord lift in curls from an aluminum bucket in the bottom of the inflatable and feed over the gunnel, disappearing into the green depths until the orange float is pulled out of the dinghy and bobs in the water. He repeats this process with the remaining trap, then rows back to his ketch and Orion.

Six hours later, standing in the cockpit, he inhales the mixed fragrances of salt air and pine forest while somewhere in the shallows behind him a great blue heron squawks. He looks toward Charlotte Rose's house and garden but doesn't see her and is sorry not to at least catch a glimpse of her.

He climbs down the stern ladder into his inflatable telling Orion to stay. A breeze across the cove drives small waves that gently rock the dinghy. He rows toward his first crab trap, favoring his left shoulder, the oars creaking in their locks on every pull. Making long reaches forward, he sweeps backwards with the oars, propelling the dinghy ahead, leaving tiny eddies in the water from each oar blade. After every stroke, he lets the inflatable glide until it almost stops, and in only half a dozen pulls he's at his first trap.

He takes in the orange float and pulls up the yellow cord. Sunlight slants down from behind him and he sees the trap rising from the depths like a strange metallic sea animal, its image wavering in the translucent green water. When a mound of yellow cord accumulates in the bottom of the dinghy, the trap breaks from the surface, and he lifts the dripping wire mesh into the boat.

Disappointment. Three Dungeness and a Red crab, all except one Dungeness too small to keep. He pulls a thick rubber glove onto his right hand and withdraws the small Dungeness, their legs and claws moving wildly. One at a time, he drops them over the side, watching them descend into the depths. When he reaches into the trap for the Red crab, it manages to clamp one claw on his gloved hand. With a wave of his arm, he shakes the crab free, and it arcs out from the dinghy, plopping into the water. He scoops seawater into a yellow plastic pail and drops the legal-size crab's knobby red body into the bucket.

Concerned now, he rows a hundred yards into the wind to his red float, anxious to see what the second trap holds. "One Dungeness does not make a crab dinner," he mutters, glancing at the yellow pail.

A sudden flash of silver startles him as a school of anchovy rises from the water, their tiny bodies thrashing, before falling back. An instant later, a harbor seal surfaces, blowing air. The seal studies Michael, its gray head glistening in the sunlight, then rolls over and sinks beneath the water. He recalls an old fisherman in Alaska telling him that seeing a seal before you raise a trap is good luck. "Let's hope that old salt was right," he mutters.

At the last float, he lets the inflatable coast to a stop, grabs the float cord and begins pulling up the dripping line. His right arm strains against the unseen weight below. In the lee of the dinghy, he peers into the translucent water and watches the trap rise shimmering from the depths. Even before the cage breaks the surface, he sees a Red and two Dungeness and all of them appear larger than the spread of his outstretched hand. Keepers!

Charlotte

After three days, she abandons hope of his returning to her dock and pushes down her disappointment. She would like to learn more about the strange life he leads and spend time with him. But as he hasn't returned, she puts Michael Cordero out of her mind and resumes working down her project list, taking advantage of the solitude that will disappear when Ben and Tommy return.

In the late afternoon he does appear, this time finding her in the vegetable garden. Her back has been turned from the water for almost an hour as she plants rows of leeks and romaine lettuce seeds. Glancing up from the rich soil, she's surprised to find him standing outside the deer fence. He's clean-shaven now and wearing fresh clothes, a blue denim shirt open at his neck and tan deck shoes under a pair of corduroy pants. He's managed to comb his rebellious hair into place although the breeze is already ruffling it loose.

"You and Orion are back," she says.

"And you're still in your garden."

"Growing season is short this far north," she says, rising. "It's now or never."

"I envy your green thumb," he says, gesturing toward her rows of young plants.

She's pleased at this compliment. He looks at her with the same intensity he brought three days ago, and she feels herself stirred again. Yet as he stands at the fence in clean clothes, hair less wild now, it's as if she's meeting him for the first time. Not as someone injured and needing her help but as a relaxed vision of vigor and strength.

"How's your shoulder?" she asks, brushing dirt off her gloves, then removing them.

"Healing well, I think," he says. "Maybe later you could look at it."

"Sure." She glances up at the sun, not far above the hills to the west. "Almost dinner time, but I don't have a lot in the house right now."

He shakes his head. "I was hoping to make you dinner. After what you did for me."

She stares at him, puzzled.

"I promise not to wreck your kitchen," he adds with a grin.

His smile is sweet, his voice kind.

"Not much you can do to my kitchen," she says, overcoming her surprise. "But I'm low on supplies."

He points to the cooler in his right hand. "I've brought everything we need."

Michael

He takes her initial hesitation at his offer to make dinner to be her doubts about his culinary skills. Or perhaps an unwillingness to let him invade her kitchen, something he would understand of course. After all, she barely knows him.

"All I need are two large pots of boiling water," he tells her, looking through the deer fence. "And a small pan, to melt butter."

"What's in the cooler?" she asks.

"Four legal-sized crabs I brought up from the bottom, just twenty minutes ago. And in here," he says, slipping his backpack off, "is an unopened package of Italian linguini."

She comes to her side of the deer fence, standing closer now.

"And here's a nice chardonnay I picked up in Tahiti last year," he says, removing a bottle of white wine and showing it to her through the fence. "I've been storing this in the bilge for a special occasion. Patching me up the other night was plenty special."

These pronouncements, and the sudden appearance of the wine bottle and linguini package, appear to surprise her.

"I noticed your kale is up already," he says, pointing behind her, to the far side of the garden. "A small salad would be nice to round out the meal."

"You like kale?" she asks in a voice tinged with skepticism.

"Pretty much like all greens. But I run out of them early on long passages."

"Can't ever get Ben or Tommy to touch kale," she confides.

He replaces the wine and linguini package in his backpack and faces her through the fence. "I didn't catch enough crab for four. Will they be joining us?"

Somewhere in the forest behind them a woodpecker hammers at a tree and the drumbeat carries to them across the meadow. She turns toward the sound and then back to him.

"They're fishing and camping up north," she says.

"Then four crabs will be plenty," he says, adding, "as long as we put Orion in the run out back."

***

In her kitchen, while they wait for the water to boil, he says, "Those are nice drawings on the refrigerator. Did your son make them?

"They're from last year. He keeps the newer ones in his room."

"He's a good artist. How old is he?"

"Almost twelve," she says, taking silverware to the dining table. "And tall already."

"May I ask who did that large painting in your living room?"

Her face clouds briefly as she comes back into the kitchen and leans against the sink counter. "I did," she says.

He's conscious of her next to him—her scent, part lavender and part forest, mixing with steam rising from the pots on the stove.

"I made it when I first arrived on Cambria," she adds.

"It's quite powerful," he says. "I've been drawn to it since I first saw it."

"Thank you," she says, filling water glasses.

"Tommy gets his talent from you then," he says, placing the wine bottle he brought on the kitchen counter.

She opens a drawer and hands him a corkscrew. "He's better than me. He can draw."

"Your painting has a lot of emotion in it," he says, pulling the cork from the wine bottle.

"Not everyone likes that," she says. "The fishermen and farmers here don't have much use for abstract impressionism. Neither do their wives."

"Art is an acquired taste for some," he says. "How long have you been painting?"

"I started sketching when I was young. My grandmother encouraged me."

"Not your mother?"

"My mother died after she gave birth to me."

"I'm sorry," he says, realizing he's blundered into a painful memory.

"It doesn't matter," she says, waving a hand. "If your mother dies when you're born, you don't miss her in the same way. It's only later that you realize what you don't have, when you start school and see all the other mothers. By then it doesn't hurt as much, I suppose."

He doesn't know what to say to this and is relieved when she continues.

"I became passionate about art when my grand-mère helped me discover the French Impressionists," she says. "I love Matisse and Monet. And Pissarro."

"There's a collection of Gauguin's paintings in Tahiti," he says, "that few people ever see."

"I'd like to get there someday," she says, wistfully.

The smaller pot is at a full boil now, and he sprinkles salt into the heaving water. "Time for the linguini to go in."

He breaks the pasta lengths in half, drops them into the boiling water and covers the pot. "Next the crabs," he says. "Are you squeamish?"

She shakes her head. "We put traps out in season. I love crab."

"Good," he says, dropping the crabs into the larger pot. He turns down the heat under the pasta so it won't boil over.

While she washes the kale leaves and slices a tomato, they make small talk about the changeable weather in the region, interspersed with silences as they stand in the kitchen. He sees she's not entirely comfortable with these silences, something he's used to, being alone at sea for weeks at a time. Although he speaks to Orion as if the Husky were another human being, a way to stay sane on the longest voyages.

"Pasta and crabs are ready," he announces after checking the pots, "and the butter's melted."

"I'll find two wine glasses," she says. "I can't remember the last time we had wine. Ben prefers beer."

"There's room in the world for a good beer," he says, draining the pasta into the large strainer she's given him and placing the steaming crabs on a platter.

After he brings everything to the table, he fills the wine glasses she's provided. Then he proposes a toast. Raising his glass, he says, "To your medical skills and hospitality. And to fair winds," he adds, "and smooth seas."

After hesitating, she raises her glass to his. "To fair winds and smooth seas," she echoes, "for everyone."

Charlotte

She tries to hide her surprise and pleasure at Michael Cordero's confidence and grace in her kitchen, the way he's made the meal preparation seem effortless.

"I'll get a bowl for the empty shells," she tells him. "And while I'm at it, I'll take Toby upstairs. He loves crab a little too much."

"I'll bet he does," he says.

When she returns, he lifts a large crab and a heaping pasta serving onto her plate.

By the time she sits across from him, her crab has cooled enough not to burn her fingers. Wrestling a crab cracker around one leg, she splits the shell. Using a tiny two-pronged fork, she extracts the soft, pink meat and dips it in the shared bowl of melted butter that sits between them. She savors the tender, sweet taste, a hint of brine under the butter.

Eating the crabs takes effort, and she concentrates on enjoying them. Cracking the shell, prying out the meat. The meal becomes a sensual experience, allowing the pink shells to slip from her butter-smeared fingers, then licking her fingers the way he does, across from her, with no apology. She sees him relishing each juicy morsel pulled from a cracked leg, as if a hard-won victory, then soaking them in the melted butter with a kind of reverence. Sitting across from her, he eats with a quiet gusto she finds contagious.

When they do start a conversation, she describes the challenges of raising vegetables, the battles against insects and varmints. She talks about how fast Tommy's growing up, that he already has a crush on a girl from the other side of the island. Then she tells him about home-schooling her son. How sometimes she felt at the end of her knowledge, unable to give him the answers he expects from her and the disappointment she feels in herself at those times.

"There's no school on the island?" he asks, placing an empty crab's leg in the bowl.

"A converted barn is all we have. Passes for a little one-room schoolhouse," she tells him between sips of chardonnay. Her experience is limited, but the wine he brought tastes pleasant on her tongue.

"Unfortunately, we've never been able to keep a teacher for more than one or two years. Too isolated out here. Not enough for a young person to do, and little chance of finding a suitable partner. A few older teachers came out to the island. But they didn't last long either with no doctor here, as you know. And it's hard teaching all the grades at one time in a single room, even with less than a dozen students."

She realizes she's running on while he remains silent, and she thinks he must be bored with her mundane island life. But he's concentrating on her words, his eyes shining warmly, making her feel as if she's the only one that matters in his world. She finds it comforting talking to a man who listens.

After the last crab is cracked and the pink meat soaked in melted butter, they finish the linguini, and he drains the wine bottle into her glass. Already, she's feeling light-headed. She rarely has alcohol with meals, only joining Ben occasionally for a beer with dinner.

"Another toast," Michael Cordero says, raising his glass, waiting for her to do the same. "To fishing gaffs and butterfly bandages."

She laughs.

"Now your turn," he says, with a half-smile on his lips she's come to admire.

She shrugs. "I'm not used to making toasts."

He sits back in his chair. "There's no hurry."

She tries to think of something clever. But the wine and rich dinner are almost too much for straight thinking. "To Tommy's drawings," she says finally, raising her glass.

"Good one," he says, clinking glasses.

After finishing her wine, she looks at his broad face and soft eyes. With him cooking in her kitchen, it seems natural to have him here. It occurs to her to feel guilty about the evening, but she tells herself she hasn't done anything wrong.

"Are you up for a walk along the beach?" she asks, yielding to yet another impulse.

"What about the dishes?"

"Dishes can wait," she says, rising from the table. "We shouldn't waste the light. I'll look at your shoulder. Then we'll go outside."

Michael

He removes his shirt and straddles a chair, a ritual that's become familiar now, a peculiar kind of intimacy between them. He watches her place the laundry basket on the kitchen counter and search for the things she needs. Her sweater rides up, and when her long hair slides to one side, a melon-slice of skin, smooth and inviting, shows above the top of her jeans.

She moves behind him, and he feels the scissors' cold metal as she cuts away the gauze. "Please don't move," she says. "I wouldn't want to cut you."

He flinches when she pulls off a strip of adhesive tape slowly, tearing away the hairs underneath.

"That must hurt," she says, tracing with cool fingers an outline of the exposed area.

"I have a pretty high pain threshold," he says. "But you might try pulling the adhesives off faster."

"I can do that," she says. With quick motions, she tears off the remaining strips. "Better?"

"Much."

As she works on his wound, her fingers are soft on his skin.

He hears her unscrew the cap on the rubbing alcohol, feels the cold sting as she flushes the wound, her breath powdery on his neck. Closing his eyes, he inhales her scent, and when she leans closer, her hair brushes his arm.

"You can put your shirt on," she says, softly. "The wound is healing well, but there'll be a scar. I'm afraid you should have had some stitches."

He retrieves his shirt from the back of the chair. "Preferable to bleeding to death," he says. "I can live with a scar."

He stands in the middle of the dining room and buttons his shirt, then pushes the shirttail into his jeans, trying not to feel self-conscious, aware that he wants to reach for her. Instead, he's drawn to the flecks of jade in her eyes. Sailing around the Pacific he'd met women but was never interested enough to stay anchored in one place. Something about his experience with Charlotte Rose is different. Maybe he's imagined it, but a hidden intensity simmered underneath their conversation during dinner, an intensity evident in her living room painting.

"If we're going to do that walk, we better head out now," she says, drawing him from his thoughts.

He nods. "It'll do Orion good. Me too."

Charlotte

In late-April this far north, it stays light until well after eight o'clock. She leads him across the meadow and down to the water where they walk below the driftwood berm that winter storms have tossed high up on the beach. Behind the sand, madrona trees lean toward the water, their orange bark and elegant branches striking in the setting sun.

They fall into step with each other, and she turns to him. "You mentioned three days ago your boat was knocked down. What happened exactly?"

He flings an oblong piece of driftwood down the beach that Orion races after and then carries back to them in his mouth. "A squall hit us, right after the gaff went into me. The worst timing." He takes the driftwood from Orion and throws it again. "The masts were almost in the water, and my spinnaker blew out. Chaos inside the boat of course. Everything not bolted down went flying."

"Sounds bad," she says.

"I've spent a lot of time cleaning up the interior."

"Resting too, I hope."

"Enough," he says. "But I need to focus on what really needs doing."

"What's that?" she asks, curious.

Orion runs back to them, the piece of driftwood in his mouth. Michael takes it from him, and, with his good right arm throws it far down the beach again.

"Repair the spinnaker. And go up the mast to check the rigging," he tells her. "Then dive the boat to see if she suffered any damage coming over that reef at the entrance. Make certain she's seaworthy, before I go back out."

Hearing this, that Michael Cordero can't just raise his anchor and sail away, that there's much more to be done, she feels relief, grateful she can spend more time with him.

As they walk side by side into the on-coming dusk, the water laps against the stone and sand beach, a sound she finds soothing. This time she's the one who throws the driftwood stick for Orion to race after.

"Can you do that work with an injured shoulder?" she asks.

"I'll start with the spinnaker repair. See if it's possible to salvage it. That'll give my shoulder more time to heal."

A bald eagle glides over the cove with a wriggling salmon in its talons. She's seen this so many times, it doesn't surprise her, after all the bay is named Eagle Cove for a reason. But Michael turns and follows the eagle's flight across the water until it lands in the tallest tree on the far shore.

"That nest has been active as long as I've been here," she tells him.

"Impressive," he says, turning back to her.

"What's involved in repairing the spinnaker?"

"Mostly taping and sewing," he answers, bending down to pull the driftwood piece from Orion's mouth. But this time, the Husky doesn't want to let go.

He straightens up and asks, "You wouldn't by any chance have a sewing machine I could use?"

She tries to hide her surprise as they continue along the water.

"I've never had a man ask to use my sewing machine," she says in a teasing voice. "And you don't seem the least bit self-conscious about it."

He laughs. "Sail lofts charge a fortune. Over the years, I've tried to repair *Shearwater's* sails myself."

"How long has that been?" She wonders if she's asking too many questions.

A shadow crosses his face. "Since my wife died, and I built *Shearwater*."

"I'm so sorry," she says in a soft voice. Her face flushes up to her hairline. "I didn't know."

A sound emerges from his throat, but no words.

His wife is dead, and he's alone. As they walk down the beach, she feels torn, thinking he's free to find someone, but she's a married woman and shouldn't be having such thoughts. It should be none of her business whether he has a wife, or not. But she can't deny it matters to her. And she wonders if that makes her an awful person.

"How did your wife die?" she asks before she can stop herself. "If it's okay to ask."

The sound of the waves lapping at the sand fills the silence after her question.

Orion finally tires of the driftwood game and takes his place between them.

"I can talk about it now," Michael says slowly, his voice lowering as they walk. "Couldn't for the longest time."

As the slow dusk descends around them, a few stars appear above the eastern horizon.

"You must have loved her deeply."

"She was everything to me."

She realizes he's talking about a relationship at least a dozen years in the past, yet she hears deep sorrow in his voice now.

Reaching the end of the beach, they turn around and walk back toward the house, Orion ranging far ahead.

"Djanette went into cardiac arrest during surgery," he says in a voice so quiet she strains to hear him above the lapping waves. "While I was in the war, she wanted to correct a deformed leg she was born with, that caused her to walk with a serious limp. She didn't write to me about the operation. Not a word about it in any of her letters." He reaches down for a flat stone and skips it across the water. It hops three times, leaving radiating circles on the surface.

As they resume walking, she's not sure he'll continue. A flock of sanderlings land on the beach, and Orion runs at them. Before he can reach them, they fly off, peeping.

"We'd been corresponding the whole time I was overseas. But she was afraid that if I started worrying about her while I was in combat, something would happen to me. That's the kind of person she was."

He reaches down and throws another flat stone across the water, harder this time. Four skips. Four radiating circles, each one smaller than the last.

"I didn't care about her limp. It never bothered me, but I know it bothered her. She didn't want to be pitied."

He falls silent again.

"Afterwards, I tried to drink myself to death. But I pulled out of it long enough to realize there was one thing that still had meaning for me. To build *Shearwater*, my father's last design before he died, and to spend time crossing oceans under sail. Something I'd dreamed about since I was a boy."

His words stir her, and she tries to think of what to say.

Orion runs past them, charging down the beach in the opposite direction.

"Where did you go once you built her?" she asks.

He glances out at the water, then turns back to her. "After stopping in the Caribbean, I sailed to Cartagena, where I spent a year. I loved that Old City. It felt like I'd lived there in an earlier life, it seemed so familiar. Long narrow streets, colorful buildings, warm people."

"Do you speak Spanish?"

"I picked it up during my eighteen months in Spain, when I went to visit my father's family near Barcelona and stayed on as a stringer for the Boston Gazette, covering the Spanish civil war. That's how I started writing. As a journalist."

She thinks about the exotic life he's led. He appears to want to talk now, his voice more animated. She wants to know as much as she can about him and is filled with questions.

"Where did you go after Cartagena?"

"South, to the Falkland Islands and around Cape Horn," he says. "Up to Ecuador and then across the Pacific, to French Polynesia. Much later, a tough slog up to Alaska. And then down the Inside Passage, the west coast, Mexico and back to Ecuador."

"That's an extraordinary voyage," she says, trying to imagine traveling such a long distance on a boat the size of the one she can see by glancing to her right, as they walk down the beach.

"Been sailing that same loop around the Pacific for a while now. Looking for something I haven't found yet, I guess."

"All that time at sea?"

"Mostly," he says.

She thinks about this. There's a strength about this man walking beside her, a confidence and self-reliance that allows him to cross oceans on a small boat by himself. Yet to her, there is something fractured, something hidden in his expression, a contrast that intrigues her. She supposes it has to do with the war and losing his wife. There's an unmistakable sorrow in his eyes at times.

As they reach the house, she turns to him. "I have an old Singer sewing machine my mother left me. Would that be any help?"

"Could be," he says. "Worth a try."

"I could sew for you," she offers.

"I appreciate that," he says. "But I could try it myself rather than burdening you."

There's that self-reliance again, she thinks.

"Assuming," he says, "you'll trust me with a keepsake from your mother?"

"I trust you," she says, before she can think about it. "You didn't wreck my kitchen."

They laugh together. "I'll bring the sail ashore in the morning, and we can have a go at it. Will that work?"

"That'll be fine," she says, as they reach the porch steps.

"What about the dishes?" he asks.

"You cooked. I'll clean."

"Thanks," he says with a smile. "Come on, Orion," he shouts to the Husky. Before he turns away, he says, "Thank you for a lovely evening, Charlotte. I'll see you in the morning."

* * *

Back in her kitchen, standing at the sink window, she can just see Michael in the day's last light as he rows back to his boat. She's learned so much more about him and his life, and the exotic places he's been. The entire day went by without her thinking about Ben. She wonders again if she should feel guilty about that, and about the dinner she shared with Michael. *I haven't done anything wrong* she tells herself again. *I'm being friendly, helping a veteran of the war with a boating injury.*

Rinsing the pots, she believes there's nothing more involved, but the question of where this is leading, and that it could be leading somewhere, stays with her.

Michael

In the morning, he rows the dinghy towards Charlotte's dock, putting his back into it but still going easy on his left shoulder. A high cloud cover stretches away to the edges of sky—a speckled cirrocumulus pattern suggesting to him that the weather might change.

Two empty five-gallon water jugs and the plump spinnaker bag sit in the stern, his backpack and Orion in the bow. Only a gentle breeze stirs, and he's thankful for that—little wind means he can spread the spinnaker on the meadow below her house without it blowing all over her property. Pulling on the oars, he sees a family of otters swimming a dozen yards away, their faces turned to him in curiosity before they dive under the water.

He reaches her dock in a dozen pulls and is pleased at how little discomfort he feels in his left shoulder now. Thanks to her aid, the wound is healing fast and with no infection. Shipping the oars and tying up at the dock, he's eager to see her.

She's not in her garden this time but comes out onto the porch as he strides up the path carrying the spinnaker bag, his backpack draped over his right shoulder, Orion trailing behind.

"Spinnaker day," she says, coming out to the railing.

"And a beautiful one on the island this morning."

She's pulled her hair into a ponytail that drapes down her back, and she's wearing a newer pair of jeans. They show off the flare of her hips and her legs. A short-waisted shirt tied over her stomach leaves a bit of bare skin showing. She looks younger than she did yesterday. And there's a glow on her cheeks that wasn't there the morning after his accident.

"How can I help?" she asks, leaning over the railing.

"I could use a couple of large tarps," he says, setting the spinnaker bag on the bottom step and sliding his backpack off. Orion moves into the shade of the house and lies down.

"Let's try the shop," she says.

"I'll just tie Orion to the porch where he can rest in the shade."

Then they walk a dirt path to a barn-like building behind the house.

"Sorry for how this looks," she says when they're inside. "Always adding things but nothing ever comes out. Quite the mess."

Glancing around, he takes in the disorganized state of the shop. It's not how he would keep things. But every person has their own way of storing tools and supplies, he tells himself.

"There's a pile of tarps in that corner," she says, pointing.

He searches through the stack. "These two will do."

Out on the meadow, they spread the green tarps over the grass and weight the edges with rocks. He hands her one corner of the spinnaker, and together they pull the red cloth from its bag. Even in almost no wind, the sail billows until they pull it tight and weight it with stones.

"This fabric is so thin," she says, holding one corner. "The sails on my dad's boat were thick and stiff, like cardboard."

"Before synthetic fabrics," he says. "Did your dad have a spinnaker."

She shakes her head no.

"You use a spinnaker only in light air," he tells her. "And only when you're sailing in the same direction as the wind. When that squall hit, it was way too much wind for this sail. Blew it out. Like popping a giant balloon."

She puts the corner of the sail down. "What's next?"

"I'll tape it just enough," he says, "to make it easier to sew the tears."

"It's a gorgeous, rich color," she says.

"I like it too. Spectacular when it's flying. Like a huge red kite."

"What's that soaring bird on it?"

"Take a guess," he says.

After a few seconds, she hazards, "A shearwater?"

"You got it!" he says, grinning. "They're remarkable long-distance flight birds. Can stay aloft over the sea for months at a time, sleeping and eating without ever touching down."

"That's stunning."

"They make long migrations, circling the Pacific Ocean."

"Like you've been doing," she says.

"Part of me wants to be a shearwater," he says, quietly. "Sailing alone and not stopping."

He sees her hesitate, as if she can't decide something. "Well, I like the sound of the word…shearwater."

"So do I."He points to the spinnaker lying on the tarp. "If you're willing to hold the edges of these tears together I'll do some taping," he says, indicating a long tear that almost splits the sail in half.

She kneels on the tarp and joins the edges of the ripped sail.

From his backpack, he removes a shears and two rolls of sail tape, one wide, one narrow.

"I could tape all these rips," he tells her. "But the sail will last a lot longer if it's sewn." He gestures for her to pull the sail tight and begins taping as she feeds him the joined edges.

After twenty minutes of spot taping, he gathers up the sail and carefully stuffs it back into its bag, then turns to her. "Thank you. I couldn't have done this by myself."

"Of course," she says, leading him up the porch steps to the sewing room.

Inside the house, they pass through the living room. The large painting on the wall behind the couch begins to make more sense to him. The vivid swirls and thrusts of color suggest not only the sadness he sensed in the painting when he woke in her living room that first morning, but also the vitality and spirit he saw in her eyes during their dinner and walk last night.

Charlotte

"There it is," she says, pointing to her mother's sewing machine sitting on a small table in the catch-all room. She pulls out the single matching chair and removes the cloth cover on the machine. "A lot of years on it. But it still works well, for me."

She watches as he takes a section of the sail from the bag and lays the fabric out flat on the sewing machine platform. "I carry my own sail thread with me," he says, sitting down at the table. "Thin enough for this light fabric, but still strong."

"Should I leave you to it?" she asks.

"Maybe you can hang around a bit in case I get into trouble?" he asks. "If you can spare the time."

"I can stay a while," she says, standing behind him.

He removes a spool of red thread from his backpack and installs it on the machine. Slowly, he runs the fabric under the needle as the Singer chatters loudly. She watches as he sews one long tear and then starts on another. He's unhurried and careful and doesn't appear to be at all self-conscious as he sews.

She's certain not a single man on this island, nor any of Ben's commercial fishing friends, would go anywhere near a sewing machine. Coming from San Francisco in 1946 she had been shocked at learning how rigid the roles for men and women were on the island, and not much had changed since then.

But after everything she's learned about the strange life Michael Cordero has led since the war, and with him sitting at her mother's sewing machine now, it's clear to her how different he is from any of these men. He's saying in effect to her, to anyone, I don't fit the usual molds. This is who I am, and I'm not changing myself to fit what some think is the role of a man in this world.

This is what she imagines him saying as she stands over him. She feels an urge to run her fingers through his thick mane of hair, but she pushes it down amid the sewing machine's noise.

"What do you think?" she asks, leaning over him for a closer look.

"This should work," he says, as he pushes more fabric forward through the needle.

"I'm learning about sail repair," she says. "You never know when that might come in handy."

He laughs. "There won't be a lot of sailboats coming in here. But you could make a good living on the mainland."

"I think I'll stay with gardening," she says.

He looks up and smiles warmly, a smile to which she's increasingly drawn. "I appreciate the loan of your mother's Singer," he says. "This is really working well."

"I'm glad," she says.

Then he turns back to the machine and resumes feeding the bright red fabric through the stuttering needle.

***

Late in the morning, from the orchard where she's trimming tree branches, she sees him come through the front door, carrying the spinnaker bag onto the porch.

"All done?" she calls, leaning her loppers against a tree trunk and moving through the orchard gate.

"Just have to finish taping over the stitching," he says, coming down the porch steps and meeting her halfway.

"When you're done, I should have a look at how that shoulder's healing one more time." She tells herself it's only attending to his wound that drives this suggestion, but she knows it could be wanting again to feel her fingers on his bare skin.

"Fair enough," he says, "although it's feeling good now."

***

An hour later, when he's seated with his back facing her, she studies the curve of his spine where it disappears into his jeans. Seeing his bare torso now is different from when he was lying unconscious on her living room floor. She questions if she's using his wound as pretext to undress him. She reaches over to remove the small gauze bandage, but her elbow knocks over the tulips on the end table. The vase crashes to the floor, sending flowers and water scattering. She flushes as he turns and kneels to help gather the flowers.

"I don't know how that happened," she says, embarrassed.

"Oh good, the vase didn't break," he says, in a calm voice.

She brings a thick towel to mop up the water, aware of his being half-naked alongside her as he picks up the last of the long-stemmed tulips.

When the vase is refilled, and the tulips arranged again, she places the flowers on the kitchen counter out of harm's way. Then she returns to where he's patiently sitting. She moves around behind him and carefully examines his back. "I don't think there's anything more I can do," she tells him. "It's well on its way to being healed. Doesn't need any more bandaging."

"I owe you," he says, rising and taking his shirt from the back of the chair.

She shakes her head. "That crab dinner last night was payment in full."

"I enjoyed sharing that," he says, buttoning his shirt and tucking it into his jeans.

He moves toward the front door. "I was thinking of making sandwiches," she offers. "We could take them with us on a hike up Keller Peak. I could show you some of what I love about that mountain. That is if you don't need to be back at your boat right away."

Toby pads across the living room and rubs against Michael's leg. She watches him reach down and pet the Siamese's soft coat. "He likes you," she says.

"I like cats," he replies. "I'd have one, but on boats they're not as practical as a dog. And Orion is good security when I go ashore in a new anchorage for the first time."

She waits to see if he'll respond to her invitation to hike Keller Peak, thinking maybe Toby has provided a distraction that allows him to decline without seeming to.

"I'd like to see some of this island before I leave," he says.

She's pleased he'll go with her, but when he says *before I leave*, it's hard for her to pull in a breath.

Michael

At the trailhead to Keller Peak, Orion sniffs the trunks of the giant cedars and firs on either side of the clearing. Before they left the house, Charlotte changed into shorts and a T-shirt, warning him it would be a warm hike. Now seeing her bare legs, he tries to keep from staring but it's difficult.

As they start up the duff-covered trail, a woodpecker is hammering hard into a tree trunk, and warblers and wrens twitter around them. As Charlotte predicted, the overcast has burned off, letting shafts of sunlight filter down through the vaulted canopy, heating the trail.

At first the path is wide enough to hike side by side through the old growth forest. But when the trail narrows, Charlotte moves ahead, and they hike single file on flat ground. Walking behind her, he notes her assured stride. She must hike this trail often, he thinks.

Sword ferns and dense salal line the trail on both sides. Before the path begins its upward angle, it passes through a low wet place where the scent of Indian plum fills the air and for a few minutes, he forgets his labored breathing. He loves wooded stands like these—the fertile smell of peat, flashes of cloud-dappled sky through the leaves, the humbling sense of his own small size among these ancient trees.

When the trail becomes steeper, Charlotte pulls ahead of him. He wills himself to move faster, but his breath comes in gasps now and his legs rebel. The pitch of the trail increases even more as it angles off to the left, following the contour of the mountain and the distance to Charlotte's bobbing pack grows. He feels faintly ridiculous not being able to match her pace. In his early twenties, before the war, he summited half a dozen of Colorado's "fourteeners," real mountains with thin air and steep exposure. Keller Peak, by contrast, couldn't be more than twelve hundred feet high. But the accident and his blood loss have caught up with him. His lungs ache.

Charlotte scurries up this steeper section with the agility of a deer. But finally, she must realize he hasn't kept up with her and turns to look back down the trail. Feeling foolish, he waves and sees her break into a smile.

When she and Orion come down the path to where he's leaning against the trunk of a cedar, she says, "I lost you."

He pulls in a breath and reaches for Orion. The Husky's fur smells of trail dust, his muzzle damp from exertion. He encircles the Husky with his arms, feeling a wet tongue on his face. "I was hoping for a tour of the island," he says, rising. "Not a re-enactment of the Bataan death march."

She lets out a rich, unrestrained laugh. The kind of laugh he hasn't heard from a woman in a long time.

"They go slower in a Marine hazing," he adds.

Her mouth forms a wide grin and her green eyes flash in the sunlight. For the first time since he arrived, she seems free of whatever burdens she carries. And already on this hike, he's become aware there's more to her than he's given her credit. Drawn to nature. Something untamed.

"This is my normal pace," she says. "I tend to lose myself in reverie coming up this particular trail."

He rubs Orion's head and pats his flanks. "I'm embarrassed I can't keep up with you."

"You're still missing a lot of blood," she says in an understanding voice. "Let's go back down. There's something else I want to show you."

"Down is good," he agrees.

He follows her for half a mile to where the trail leaves the mountain's shoulder and enters a dense stand of alders, the air immediately cooler. A few hundred yards in, she turns onto a path so faint he'd missed it on the way up. Pushing their way through ferns and vines, they climb over fallen logs and around large rocks. They skirt a fallen cedar, the huge root system upturned and unnatural in its exposure. Scents of tree bark and lichen rise like a mist all around them. He's awed by the beauty of this place.

They emerge into a clearing where a stream bubbles over moss-encrusted rocks, then tumbles from a granite ledge into a shimmering pool. Orion runs over and laps at the water. Huge shafts of yellow sunlight slant down through the tree canopy surrounding the clearing.

In the filtered light he turns to her. "This is amazing."

"I treat myself to this spot on the way down." She slips the pack off her shoulders and lets it slide to the ground. "I brought an axe up here last year," she says, pointing behind him. "Made myself a bench."

A centuries-old cedar lies where it crashed to the forest floor, its upper half charred by a long-ago lightning strike. He sees she's carved a long seat into the horizontal trunk.

She motions for him to sit while she bends to her pack. "Your sandwich," she says, handing him double slabs of brown bread holding slices of gouda and large lettuce leaves. "I brought bottles of Orange Crush we can stick in the stream. Water's plenty cold here."

He wedges the bottles between rocks under the water, then sits next to her, facing the waterfall, savoring the first bite of his sandwich. Orion has circled the clearing, sniffing at rocks and shrubs. He trots over, and Michael breaks off a piece of bread and feeds it to him.

"Does anyone else ever come here?" he asks.

"Less than two dozen families live on the island. I'm not sure anyone else knows this spot. It's well hidden. Tommy came up here with me a few times when he was younger."

He sweeps a hand around the clearing. "It's mesmerizing."

"Special, for sure," she says, between bites of sandwich.

They eat in silence, listening to the bird calls around them.

"Do you know the birds we're hearing?" he asks.

"Mostly juncos and nuthatches. White-crowned sparrows and northern flickers," she tells him. "Robins and warblers, of course."

"Quite the symphony."

"The forest is so quiet you can hear the birds from a long distance. That doesn't happen in a city."

Orion flops down between them, panting.

After a while, Michael retrieves the sodas and opens them with his Swiss army knife. He hands one to her and takes a sip from his bottle, glancing at the waterfall and the immense trees surrounding them. That she loves a setting like this reveals so much about her. It makes him believe she'd be drawn to the sea's beauty, and to sailing. He feels the same contentment here as he does at sea, on days when the ketch almost sails herself, gliding over rolling waves in a stiff breeze under a transparent sky.

The world is a beautiful place, he thinks, if you know where to look, and clearly Charlotte Rose knows where and how to look.

He glances at her again as she sits cross-legged on the cedar bench, radiant in a shaft of sunlight. Something ancient stirs inside him then, a longing, a desire to counter his loneliness and wrap his arms around this lovely woman. He tries to push down these feelings. She's a married woman, with a son. *Don't become interested or attached*, he warns himself.

But something profound is leading him toward her. He's not sure he has the will or desire to fight what is happening in this lush forest, rooted in ancient rock, surrounded by an expansive sea, her hair a red crown of sunlight.

There are times, he believes, when you must let the current of your life sweep you along, like a boat caught in a flooding tide.

To find out where the current takes you.

And what awaits when you arrive.

Charlotte

Sitting on the cedar bench, she's reminded of a time she brought Tommy to this clearing, soon after she found it. He was only six. The first thing he did, before she could stop him, was rush under the waterfall, drenching all his clothes. Rather than scold him, she waded into the pool with him, under the falling sheets of water. Tommy laughed and laughed, his joy palpable, and they romped and played in the water for an hour, then two.

This waterfall play, and other activities like it, bound the two of them together in a strong mother-son relationship. Only in the last few years has Tommy begun to draw away from her, towards Ben. She understands this is a natural evolution for her son, but that doesn't make it any less hard.

When she unfolds her legs and rises from the bench, Orion rubs against her. She reaches down to pat the Husky's head before re-shouldering her pack. Gathering the long sweep of her hair with both hands, she lifts it from her neck, then lets the mass of it fall back over her shoulders and the pack, conscious of Michael looking at her.

While they rested in her hideaway, he appeared to study her in his watchful, quiet way, an alertness on his face, qualities she'd expect in someone who spends months or even years at sea. Feeling his eyes on her that way isn't something she's used to, and she wonders what he's thinking.

Starting down toward the trailhead, she considers inviting him to dinner. She tells herself it would be paying him back in kind, for his cooking. But what kind of signal might it send to him about her intentions? *If only I knew what my intentions are*, she thinks, *and where to draw the line.*

As they descend, she feels excited and reckless at the same time. "It's my turn to make dinner," she tells him when the trail widens, and they can walk side-by-side.

He doesn't respond right away. She imagines him working through the implications.

She thinks about the implications too, as they pass through a stand of moss-covered firs, Orion running ahead of them. What would Ben think about her inviting this man to dinner while he and Tommy are away? She's only planning a simple soup, she tells herself, nothing fancy. And Michael Cordero has behaved like a gentleman the whole time he's been with her. Reckless or not, she wants to make him dinner.

"I appreciate the invitation," Michael says, turning to her. "What can I bring?"

"Only Orion," she tells him.

They walk more slowly now, among bracken and giant sword ferns that rise out of the understory.

"What time?" he asks.

"Six would be good."

The trail descends around a marshy pool, dank-smelling and populated with Indian lilies and skunk cabbages—their brilliant yellow tongues reaching to taste the afternoon air.

"Looks like the sun's going away again. Would you mind if I use your shower before dinner?"

"I've wondered what you do about bathing on the boat," she responds.

"On sunny days, I heat water in a black rubber bag on deck," he says. "Then I hang the bag in the tiny shower compartment. Or in the cockpit if I want more room."

"That doesn't sound like much of a shower," she says.

"You can't waste water at sea, so you learn to make do," he says. "But I am getting low on fresh water and wondered if I could fill a few five-gallon jugs?"

A ruby-throated hummer hangs suspended near them—its wings a blur—before it darts up into the trees.

"We have a good well," she says, "take as much as you need. And you can use all the water you want tonight for your shower."

"That'll be a luxury," he says. "You'll have to pry me out."

She laughs. "Hopefully, the dinner I'm planning will take care of that."

***

After he rows back toward *Shearwater,* and she's certain he and Orion are on the ketch, she goes out to Ben's shop. Behind stacks of lumber and half-empty paint cans, against the back wall, is the wide six-drawer dresser Ben felt was too big for the house. It was another keepsake from her mother, trucked from storage in California and then barged to the island after she and Ben were married.

She grabs a cloth and wipes off layers of dust and cobwebs from the top of the dresser, then kneels and opens the second drawer from the bottom. Piece by piece, she removes some of the clothes she'd brought with her from San Francisco and places them on the clean dresser. She takes out a blue short-sleeved summer dress cut low at the neck, a long heavy coat she wore on chillier days on the Bay, two pairs of expensive jeans and several checkered cotton blouses, beige or grey toned.

In the bottom drawer, underneath another layer of clothes, she finds the sandalwood box with her jewelry, none of which she's ever worn on the island. "Too fancy for Cambria Island," had been Ben's comment early in their relationship when she put on some pearl earrings and a silver necklace. That's when she'd put the jewelry in the bottom drawer of the dresser.

Selecting the pale blue summer dress, a blouse, and a pair of near-new jeans, she carries them with the sandalwood box to the house, upstairs to the master bedroom. She spreads everything on the king-size bed, and Toby jumps onto the bed, sniffing at the clothing before curling up on one of the pillows. These are all the clothes Ben had told her were too frilly for the island. His exact words were "You'll embarrass us." *Embarrass you* had been her thought at the time. These were clothes that had made her feel pretty at the art school in San Francisco and now, with Michael Cordero's arrival, she finds herself wanting to feel that way again.

Holding the blue dress and looking in the full-length mirror behind the bedroom door, she wonders if the dress could still fit. Over the years she's taken care to stay trim. The extra pounds she gained carrying Tommy had melted off as she gardened, developed their orchard, and hiked Keller Peak. In contrast, Ben had continued to gain weight over time and now sported a sizable belly.

She tries on the blue dress and is pleased she can still wear it, though it's a bit tight in the bust, and more revealing of her butt than it once was. That's okay, she tells herself.

In the late afternoon, she soaks in a hot bath and then puts on the summer dress again and studies herself in the full-length mirror. Is the dress appropriate? Will Michael Cordero think she's putting on airs, or that she's dressing for him? "Well, you are doing that, aren't you," she says under her breath. Toby looks up before curling into himself again. "I don't care," she says to her Siamese.

She spends extra time brushing her long hair, then pulls it through a ring and lets the single thick column fall behind her. Her hair had always drawn compliments from Ben. It seemed to be what he most liked about her appearance, and he was never in favor of her shortening it, even though that would simplify her life and be more practical in every way.

Looking through her makeup drawer, she finds the face powder is dried out and the other cosmetics too old to be usable, all of it dating from when she left San Francisco, perhaps the last time she wore makeup.

Six o'clock comes and goes as she works on dinner. She stands back from the kitchen counter for a moment and surveys her preparations, wondering about Michael's taste in food and whether he's eaten in some great restaurants at stops in his voyages. She feels insecure suddenly about the simple meal she's making.

It's a warm evening and she's left the front door open. Toby scratches at the screen door, but she doesn't dare let him out. Either of the eagles resident in the cove's highest cedar could carry Toby off as if he weighed nothing, and she'd never see him again.

By six-thirty she starts to think Michael Cordero is going to stand her up, making the nature of the meal she's planned a moot point.

Then, through the kitchen window, she sees him rowing fast toward her dock. "He didn't forget," she whispers.

She watches him whipping the oars forward and back, the inflatable flying across the water. His shoulder is healing well, she thinks. And then he's running across the dock ramp and up the path, Orion romping along beside him.

"I'm so sorry," he says when he reaches the front door, breathing fast, "I fell asleep after I tried out the spinnaker."

"I was beginning to worry," she says, bending over to rub Orion behind his ears.

When she straightens up, he says, "Your dress is beautiful."

She can tell from his eyes he means it, and she feels pleased he's noticed.

"How did the sail work?" she asks.

"Just fine, thanks to your mom's sewing machine." He removes his windbreaker and lays it across a living room chair. "I appreciate your help taping it."

"I didn't do much," she says, wondering why she's always so self-effacing around this man. "You still want to take that shower?"

"If I'm not ruining dinner. I brought some clean clothes in my backpack."

"Dinner can coast for a while," she says, leading him to the kitchen. "And I'm still working on a salad. It's up the stairs and down the hall. Second door on the right. I put out fresh towels, and you'll see soap and shampoo."

"I won't be long," he says.

When she hears the water running upstairs, she resumes slicing vegetables. She thinks about him in the shower, pictures water cascading over his shoulders, running down his chest to…

Stop that, she admonishes herself. Just because Ben's not here, doesn't mean you're entitled to those kinds of fantasies. "Besides," she whispers under her breath, "if you keep thinking about Michael Cordero being naked in your shower, you might cut off a finger slicing these carrots!"

Michael

When he comes downstairs in fresh clothes, his hair is still wet, and he feels clean in a way he hasn't felt since he used the public showers in Nanaimo. He sees the table is already set, and the dining room lights are turned down. She's lit two candles in the center of the table. The house is filled with the rich aroma of fresh baked bread.

He finds her in the kitchen stirring a pot.

"Everything smells wonderful," he tells her.

She smiles. "I made a simple soup, using vegetables from my garden, and baked a sourdough loaf," she says. "I found two old bottles of wine in the root cellar. They might be vinegar by now."

"It'll be fun to find out. What can I do to help?"

"Why don't you open the first bottle to see if it's drinkable," she says, handing him the corkscrew.

Standing at the kitchen counter, he pulls the cork and pours a bit of the brown liquid into the wine glass she's given him. He wrinkles his nose. "This one didn't make it."

"Might as well try the other one," she says, filling two large bowls with soup and taking them to the table.

He pulls the second cork. "Believe it or not, this cab is drinkable," he says, holding up the wine glass, this time glowing ruby red in the kitchen light.

"That's a miracle," she says, seating herself at the dining table. "It's been down there for years."

"We'll let it breathe a few minutes," he says, bringing the bottle and two wine glasses, and taking the chair across from her.

She passes him the breadboard. "You can slice some for us."

He cuts four thin slices of the still warm bread. Inside the sourdough's dark brown crust, the loaf is filled with air holes. He passes two slices to her, and they start in on the soup.

"This is really tasty," he says.

"A good spring soup," she nods. "Not as heavy as those I make in winter."

"And your bread is delicious."

They eat in silence for a few moments. Then he pours wine into each of their glasses.

"I'll confess I can't imagine your life here, especially in the winter," he says, softly.

She takes a sip of wine. "I do a lot of reading. Winters here are good for that. We have a book exchange on the island. And I help Tommy with his schoolwork of course. That takes up a lot of my time. And there's always endless chores of course."

"Were you born on Cambria?" he asks, between spoons of soup.

"I grew up in the Bay Area, Alameda to be exact. My father and grandmother raised me. After high school I went to the San Francisco School of Art. That's where I met David, my fiancé."

"What was that like?" he asks.

"Meeting David?"

"Art school."

Her mouth turns down. "In a word," she says, "it was discouraging. Depressing really. I was one of only a few token women they admitted that year. And my instructors made it clear, in so many words, I shouldn't expect to succeed in the fine art world. At best, they said, I might find work as a commercial illustrator. If I was lucky."

He puts down his soupspoon. "Sounds like blatant discrimination."

She nods. "That was the art world then. Whatever dreams I had of becoming a fine art painter died in that school."

"I'm sorry to hear that," he says. "I wish I could say it was different in journalism, but it wasn't. At least not when I worked for the Boston Gazette, before the war. There was only one woman in the newsroom. She suffered a lot of abuse, despite what a few of us did to try to help her."

"Maybe it's changing," she says. "Living out here, I have no way of knowing."

"I'm not sure either," he says. "May I ask what happened with David?"

He sees her hesitate and her forehead furrows. "He was the one big positive thing that happened to me in art school. The way he pursued me, and his belief in my artistry, restored some of my confidence. We were engaged, but then Pearl Harbor happened."

She stops, looks down at the table, and he's not sure she'll continue.

Reaching for her glass, she takes a sip of wine and then looks up with sadness. "David enlisted in the Air Force, and after his training he was shipped to England. He served in a bomber squadron. We'd been living in an apartment in the city near the art school, but when he left for training, I moved back to Alameda with my dad and found work at a tank factory in Fremont. David's bomber went down about a week before the armistice."

He feels his throat constrict.

"We were to be married as soon as the war was over," she says, her voice filled with sorrow. "I couldn't get over the unfairness of his death."

He takes a swallow of his wine. "There's nothing fair about war," he says, softly. "For anyone." He realizes now she can empathize with his loss of Djanette.

Her eyes shadow. "It might not have even been enemy fire that brought him down," she says, with bitterness. "Our bombers were so patched together by the end of the war it's a wonder they flew at all."

It moves him that she's willing to share such painful memories.

"I'm sorry," is all he can think to say.

Was it the candlelight and wine that allows her to be this vulnerable, he wonders, or something else?

"What was it like, working in that tank factory?" he asks, attempting to take her mind off her loss.

"Drudgery," she answers. "Performing the same operation over and over, inserting bolts and tightening them, or doing spot welding. Each of us, and we were almost all women, were like tiny cogs in a giant machine."

"But you were doing your part for the war effort."

"It helped us to think so," she says, nodding. "What about your war experiences?Can you talk about them?" she asks.

He shakes his head and looks down. "I live in the present."

She drains her wine, reaches for the bottle and refills both their glasses.

"A good philosophy," she says softly. "Easy to say, harder to do."

He feels her studying him. "You're right, of course. But I've found it's the best way to live."

"You sound like a Buddhist," she says, smiling.

He doesn't answer immediately, searching for the right words, not wanting to sound pretentious. "I've read some Eastern philosophy. Crossing an ocean on a sailboat you have lots of time for reading. All religions have a core of wisdom."

"I needed some of that wisdom when I lost David," she says, "but his death cost me my faith. I was done with religion. I ran away from the life he and I had together. It was too painful going to the places we'd shared in the Bay Area."

She's staring down at her plate now. He waits.

"It's a long story," she tells him when she raises her eyes.

"We have the evening," he says, earnestly wanting to know more.

"One of my roommates in art school was from Montana. She made it sound like Eden. So, I headed there. And it was beautiful, the small town of Hamilton, the mountains around it, the skies. But the winter was brutal. So, I tried Seattle. My Dad had died in 1944, and I'd saved the money after selling his house. I felt I had time to paint before I needed to start working. But Seattle didn't appeal to me, so I went up to Anacortes. That's when I met Ben. His family homesteaded on this island in the late 1800's. He offered to let me use the cabin across the meadow. That's how I ended up here."

"There's worse places to be," he says. "Your island is spectacular."

"True, but it can feel like prison sometimes," she says, her eyes still darkened by what she's revealed to him. "You get island fever after so many years out here."

"I can understand," he says. "Sometimes in the middle of the ocean it feels that way on *Shearwater*. The boat is your whole world, and it measures just forty feet from bow to stern."

"At least we have our forests, and the mountain here," she says. "Always the mountain."

As they're finishing dinner, he asks, "How did we get so serious?"

"The wine?"

"Let's blame it on the wine."

"A convenient villain."

On an impulse he asks, "Do you like music?"

She smiles. A shy smile that intrigues him.

"Doesn't everyone?" she answers.

"I guess so."

"We have a bunch of records and an old player. I can show you what we have," she says, rising from the table. "Bring your wine. Or should I say bring the villain."

He laughs, takes up his wine glass and follows her into the living room.

Charlotte

She leads him to the cedar cabinet by the fireplace and pulls open the unpainted doors. Pointing to the albums, most in their original covers, she watches as he kneels and thumbs through the stack. She knows what's there: Patsy Cline's greatest hits, several Frank Sinatra albums, the Kingston Trio, Bill Haley and the Comets, some Bing Crosby, two Tommy Dorsey records and a Christmas album.

"A nice broad collection," he says. "I like the old crooners and the big bands."

"Patsy Kline and Frank Sinatra are my favorites," she says.

"But no Elvis," he says, in a teasing voice.

"Not yet," she says, grinning.

"Well, it's a nice collection," he repeats. "What should we play?"

She motions toward the LP stack. "You pick."

"Do you like to dance?" he asks, rising and standing close to her.

She hesitates.

In all their years of marriage, Ben has never asked her to dance. "I love dancing," she says.

"I thought I was a decent dancer," he says, "until I spent those months in Cartagena. Colombians are incredible dancers.

They'll keep you up until the small hours of the morning, even during the week. I never figured out if, or when, they slept."

"Show me," she says. *Crossing another line*, she thinks, *a bright red one*. But she can't help herself.

"Well, okay," he says, smiling. "Let's see if there's anything in this stack close to Colombian music." Crouching down, he works his way through the record covers again. She wonders what it would be like to put her arms around him. *You may find out, and then what?*

"How about this?" he says, holding up the Bill Haley record.

"I just bought that album. The guy at the record store in Bellingham said it was the start of a music revolution. It's an awfully fast tempo."

"I better push some furniture out of the way," he says. "Is that okay?"

"I'll help you," she says, taking one end of the coffee table.

When the easy chair and coffee table are moved to the walls, he takes the vinyl record from its sleeve while she waits in the middle of the room, her heart beating faster. She's going to dance with Michael Cordero. She feels dizzy, wishes she hadn't drunk so much wine.

The needle comes down on the record with a brief scratching sound, and then the opening beats of *Shake, Rattle and Roll* echo through the room. She reaches behind her head, frees her hair from the ring, and shakes it loose.

Bill Haley begins singing as Michael turns and moves toward her. She feels her pulse beating in her neck. It seems to take forever for him to reach her, as if he's been sailing toward her for a long time, and, now here, in front of her, he reaches for her hand.

A warm sensation travels up her arm as his fingers touch hers. He takes her other hand and begins to quick step her around the room. She feels awkward trying to follow. Until he arrived, she felt mostly competent, self-assured. But around him she feels awkward and ungainly. With confidence and ease, he leads her across the room, moving like a soft wind. She doesn't want to think about what she feels this near to him, and instead focuses on the music's energetic rhythm.

She follows his lead, the flowing movement of his hips and feet, and picks up the beat. He spins her under his arm, then turns her from one side to the other, brings her close, then away. Her face grows hot, her hair flies wildly, and her dress flares in a wide arc. She catches a glimpse of herself reflected in a window and likes the vibrant woman she sees there.

The next song comes on, and then another. She's breathless now as they twirl and spin.Each time he pulls her close, she inhales the soap and shampoo scents from his shower. The room rotates around her now, her world compressed into this tiny space.

Only she and Michael Cordero, dancing.

Michael

"Makes me thirsty," he says, out of breath, when *Rock Around the Clock* finishes. He's holding one of her hands but then lets her fingers slip from his.

"There's wine left, bring your glass" she says, leading him to the dining table. He follows her and pours half the remaining wine into her glass, the rest into his own. "To Columbian dancing," he says, raising his glass.

"To Bill Haley," she offers.

She moves to the kitchen, tears a paper towel off the roll next to the sink and wipes her face. "It's warm," she says, leaning against the sink counter. Her eyes are shining, her cheeks flushed. She seems happy, the way she was in the hidden glade on Keller Peak, sitting cross-legged on her carved bench under the cedars.

"That was tremendous fun," she says, taking a sip of wine. "I wish I had more albums like that one."

"What about something slower," he asks. "A change of pace."

"Try me," she says.

After they finish their wine, he thumbs through the record stack again and chooses a Frank Sinatra album. Laying the record on the turntable, he carefully lowers the needle. Coming back to her in the center of the room, he puts his left arm around her waist, ignoring the twinge in his shoulder. He takes her left hand and moves closer to her, inhaling the lavender scent in her hair. Her face glows in the soft light from the dining room candles. He's overcome by holding her this close.

They begin to sway to Sinatra's voice crooning *Where or When*, their steps becoming smaller, slower. Drawing her hand to his chest, he brings her body softly against his. He'd wondered what it would feel like to hold her. To feel her body along his. Now he knows. The most natural thing in the world. As if she's always belonged beside him.

Pulling her to him, he doesn't try to stop the response of his body, no longer fights his desire. The aloneness he's lived with all these years at sea—compounded by his shame from that night during the war in 1943, and the pain of losing Djanette—is pushed outside the circle of candlelight by her presence. After fifteen thousand blue water miles, here is a woman who could tempt him to give up the freedom that goes with endless voyaging.

At first, this realization astonishes him. Is he ready to risk loving another woman?

Slow dancing with her in the candlelight to Frank Sinatra's crooning voice, he imagines a new and different future.

Charlotte

She leans into him, light-headed from the third glass of wine, resting her head on his shoulder, her face nestled in the crook of his neck. She feels his warmth between their bodies.

They dance more slowly, in ever tightening circles, and she wonders how many other women, in far off exotic locations, he's held like this. Leading them expertly around their living rooms with the lights lowered, or on a dance floor in some night club under a reflecting mirrored ball. How many women have pressed themselves against him the way she is now, wondering what he thought about them.

They're barely moving now, although Frank Sinatra still croons *Always*. When Michael Cordero brushes against her thigh, for the second or third time this evening she wonders where they are headed? How will this end?

How do you want it to end, a voice inside asks? She doesn't know. Honestly has no answer.

For a decade, her life has been filled with small rituals and chores, one day following another. No surprises, beyond those Tommy creates for her on occasion with his drawings, or the presents he gives for her at Christmas and her birthday. Now she's dancing with this sailor off the *Shearwater*. A man who makes her senses and her body come alive and might at any moment kiss her.

And yet, there's Tommy. And Ben.

And with those thoughts, she's pulled from the moment.

Gently, Michael opens more space between their bodies as they dance. She's surprised he's so finely tuned to her mood. Even before Sinatra finishes the song, Michael lets her hand drop and slips his arm from her waist.

He moves to the record player, lifts the needle, and the room is silent.

It's so quiet now she can hear a leaping fish, somewhere out on the cove, falling back into the water with a splash. She sees from Michael's eyes that for him too, the magic of the evening has vanished.

"I didn't realize how late it is," he says.

Earlier, when he was upstairs showering, she'd wondered how the evening would end.

"I should go back to the boat," he continues. "Tomorrow's a workday."

He's a gentleman, she thinks, making a graceful exit, though she's the one who broke the spell. "What are you planning?" she asks, not wanting him to leave, but part of her knowing she should be grateful he's made that decision for her. Part of her wishing he hadn't.

"Go up the mast," he replies. "Make sure the rig wasn't damaged in the knockdown."

"Do you need help?"

He doesn't answer right away. Then he says, "It is safer and easier if someone winches me up. But I don't want to impose any more than I already have."

"You wouldn't be imposing," she says, hoping he can hear the conviction in her voice.

"It won't take long," he says. "Maybe an hour."

"I've wanted to see *Shearwater*," she says, waving a hand toward the cove. "I've never been on a sailboat like her."

"I'd be glad to show her to you. Around mid-morning?"

"I'll come out after breakfast and chores."

"Good," he says, moving towards the front door. "Thanks for the evening. Dinner was delicious."

"It was easy," she says, dismissing his compliment but appreciative at the same time. "The dancing was special. You're good, you know."

He smiles and retrieves his windbreaker. "Those Cartagena dancers deserve the credit."

At the front door, he swings on his pack and turns to her. "You picked it up fast. Made it a lot of fun," he says. "I'll see you on *Shearwater* in the morning."

When his footsteps on the porch fall silent, and she hears him call to Orion, she goes to the window and tries to follow his darkening figure down the path. But he and the Husky are soon lost in the night. Closing the window, she blows out the candles on the dining room table and turns off the kitchen lights. Upstairs in the bedroom, Toby is lying on the bedspread. She undresses in the second-floor warmth, puts on a nightgown, and lays down on the big bed, reliving the evening as she holds her Siamese and strokes his back.

She tries to bring back the magic of dancing with Michael Cordero, but thoughts of Ben intrude. Lying in bed, unable to sleep, she finds herself reliving their history.

She'd arrived in Anacortes in the Spring of 1946 and taken a small apartment in the older part of town, out by the water. For days she walked along the marshes and tidal flats, wanting to be as far from people as she could get. She didn't want to have to explain anything about her life, didn't want consolation or, worse, have to comfort consolers.

The Gudgeon Tavern was a rundown but clean bar on Second Street, near the docks, and local boat builders and fishermen hung out there. It was a short walk from her apartment, and there was something soothing about sitting at the far end of the bar and sipping a beer or two, trying to find answers to her sorrow in the tiny bubbles rising in the glass.

She began to frequent the tavern, especially when it was too rainy to go for evening walks. Since leaving California, she'd let her hair go, wasn't using any makeup, and didn't care what clothes she wore. In truth, she didn't care about anything then except nursing her bitterness that David could not only be taken from her but also so close to the war's end. Maybe for these reasons, and an aura of tragic loss she felt she projected, none of the men in the bar approached her.

Then one night, when there were no other empty seats except the one on her right, a heavy-set and bearded man sat down next to her, not saying anything. She'd seen him the evening before and guessed he was about her age. Once or twice, she caught him glancing at her in the mirror behind the bar, trying not to be obvious.

When he'd come into the tavern, several other men had greeted him warmly, in a manner indicating they knew him and liked and respected him. She guessed that with these rugged-looking men from the boatyards, you had to earn their respect with your character and capabilities, so the way they greeted this man told her something important about him.

Sitting next to her, he ordered a beer, and, at one point, his knee touched hers. He apologized profusely, clearly embarrassed. She assured him it was not a problem. He ordered a dinner of steak and potatoes and when the food arrived, he began eating with obvious pleasure.

She'd eaten almost nothing that day and now she was hungry. She turned to him and asked if the food was any good. He put down his knife and fork and looked at her, and she saw something about his eyes that reminded her of her father. When he leaned closer, she detected an odor of fish on his clothes, but his eyes were gentle, and his shyness with her obvious. She had an immediate instinct this was a man who had not spent much time around women.

"Better than you might think," he said, in a quiet voice. "There's a good cook back there." Then he surprised her by asking, "Can I order you something?"

She hesitated, wondering if she really wanted this man buying her dinner? But she thanked him and removed the worn menu card from between the ketchup and mustard bottles in front of her. After scanning the options, she told him. "I'll have the scallops with vegetables."

"Good choice," he said, adding "My name's Ben." He extended his hand which was callused and rough, another reminder of her father, who had worked his whole life in an Alameda shipyard.

"Charlotte," she said, shaking his hand.

He smiled shyly, gave her order to the bartender, and resumed eating. When her scallops came, fresh from the ocean and grilled to perfection, she enjoyed them. The first time she'd taken any pleasure in food since leaving California.

Ben finished eating and excused himself to use the bathroom. Behind the bar, serving drinks every night, was a large, affable woman who liked to tease and flirt with all the rough-looking men. Now this woman came over to her and whispered in a low voice, "He's one of the good ones."

Her face flushed at this woman's assumption, but she was pleased when Ben returned, and she didn't mind when their knees touched again as he slid onto his bar stool.

That first night, after they'd left the bar, he asked her if she wanted to go for a walk. She told him, yes, she would enjoy that. She thought it was something she could do to thank him for buying her dinner and, in truth, she didn't want to go back to her empty apartment to wallow in her sorrow.

The weather was pleasant. They walked all the way to the end of Commercial Avenue and then back, thirty blocks in all, talking in fits and bursts for a couple of hours. She learned his fishing trawler was in one of the yards undergoing a major overhaul, and that he always brought his boat to Anacortes for maintenance. That's how he knew about the good food at the Gudgeon Tavern.

He told her that work on his boat was almost completed and that he'd be returning to the small island he lived on near the Canadian border. He walked her to her apartment, and she saw that although he was rough in his demeanor, he was what her father would call a gentleman. And when Ben asked if she wanted to walk along the seawall in the morning, again she said yes.

The next day, they walked for miles, past the pilings where the old canneries had operated in Ships Cove, walking and talking, losing track of time. At first, they skirted around the topic of the war, until he told her he'd served in the Army. Because of a heart condition, he'd been given a desk job in the states. He said this in an almost inaudible voice, as if he felt guilty about not seeing combat. He told her his trawler had lain on the hard here in Anacortes for four years while he was in the Army, and that now he would start fishing again.

There was a gentleness about Ben that added to her growing trust in him, and during their walk she told him about losing David. He was the first person she'd shared this with, and she started crying. As hard as she tried, she couldn't stop her tears.

It was as if they'd been dammed up while she ran from her pain, and now the dam had finally broken. At first Ben didn't seem to know what to do. But then he made a motion to put an arm around her, and when he saw that she'd let him do that, he held her against him, and she let her tears flow until she was too exhausted to cry.

When she regained her composure and they were walking again, she told him she was trying to get far away from reminders of her life with David in California. That she wanted to go somewhere quiet and make paintings for a while. He was sympathetic and sorry she'd lost someone she loved, and understood her need to grieve, and that impressed her.

Describing Cambria Island, he told her he'd been born there and spent his whole life with only a few other kids, not having much schooling and commercial fishing at a young age, apprenticing to his father. There were no other options on Cambria, he said. You either went to the mainland, or you stayed on the island and learned to fish.

His elderly parents had moved to Arizona for the warm, dry winters and since he had no siblings, they'd given him their house and property with the understanding he would take care of them later, if they needed help. He mentioned a cabin he'd built for himself on their land, before the war. He told her she could stay in the cabin if she wanted to, and that he wouldn't charge any rent while she got herself sorted out. He blurted this out in a rush, his cheeks turning crimson above his beard as if he expected her to say no. But she didn't say no. She told him she'd think about it.

She had three days to decide, as by then his boat would be ready, and he'd be heading back to Cambria Island. Walking by the water with him on those three days, she saw further evidence that Ben was a decent man. And the way he described the island made it seem remote and beautiful, the kind of place where she could be alone and try to paint again.

When they went back to the Gudgeon for dinner that night, she heard the men tease Ben about his new red-head. She saw his embarrassment, but also a hint of pleasure at their teasing and was further reassured about what kind of man he was.

At the end of the three days, she told him she'd go with him but that he shouldn't have any expectations. He assured her he respected that and would make no demands on her. He told her there was only one tiny general store, at Limestone Bay, so she would be better off getting everything she needed here in Anacortes.

In the end, she decided to trust Ben. She understood she was taking a risk but felt she knew enough about him already to do that, and to trust her instincts. Everything pointed to him being clean, hard-working, and honest. Despite his size, and rough fisherman appearance, he'd been nothing but gentle and kind. And the allure of the island, as a place to escape to, overcame any remaining concerns she had. They loaded her suitcases and art supplies onto the *Emerald Rose* which, by now, was back in the water.

They spent all afternoon in the Safeway on Commercial Avenue, buying canned goods, pasta, cereals, and other supplies she would need on the island. And once they finished loading everything on his boat, she spent the last night in her apartment while Ben stayed on his trawler. In the morning, she paid her landlord what she owed for the balance of the month's rent, and then Ben and she left the marina in Anacortes on a sunny morning in August 1946 and motored out on the sea towards her new life on Cambria Island.

The cabin Ben had built on his parent's property turned out to be a cozy two-bedroom cottage set well back on their land, with a distant view of the water. Ben was good as his word and didn't charge her rent in the early months, and that first winter, he shared his firewood with her. In these ways, he was good to her and made her feel safe.

If she's honest with herself now, lying in the bed they share, he's been a decent and dependable husband. Before *Shearwater* coasted into Eagle Cove, she had tried to convince herself she was content, especially given the joy Tommy brought her.

Still unable to sleep, stroking Toby's soft fur, her history with Ben is something she can't easily overlook, despite the intense feelings Michael Cordero has aroused in her, since that first morning when he came out on her deck without a shirt on and locked eyes with her.

Michael

In the morning, he wakes up before sunrise, feeds Orion, and after a quick breakfast gets to work. If *Shearwater* is going to make a positive impression on Charlotte Rose, and he wants the ketch to do just that, there's much to be done before she arrives.

He's still savoring the sweetness of dancing with her, how effortless it seemed. His desire for her—the scent in her hair and her skin's warmth—remained with him last night when he returned to the ketch. Unable to sleep, he'd thought more deeply about what it might be like to sail with her, voyaging across oceans to exotic locations, the opportunity to share with her what he loves about the sea, and those far-off places. From their conversations, and everything he saw on their hike, he'd become convinced she could love that life too.

For hours, he tries to push down those thoughts, reminding himself she's married, with a son. And he wrestles with what it would mean to give up the freedom he's had all these years to go wherever the wind takes him, spending as much or as little time as he wants when he arrives. But he can't escape the feeling he and Charlotte Rose could have a rich life together. A shared life of adventure that would bring an end to the aloneness that accompanies his freedom.

Now, with the sun rising over Eagle Cove, he wants his ketch to be as inviting as possible.

"Orion, up on deck, boy!" he tells the Husky. "Can't have you below right now."

With Orion out in the cockpit, he begins scrubbing the galley, from the gimballed stove to the aluminum sink and the two large coolers set into the galley counter. He removes all the food from the coolers and wipes down their insides with a bleach solution, then replaces the provisions. Next, he cleans the settees and the dinette table. Using a soft brush, he scrubs the teak and holly floor with soap and water.

He reorganizes the captain's cabin, moving extraneous sailing gear into the V-berth, putting a new sheet on the bed, and smoothing the bedspread. Then he scrubs the toilets in both heads and cleans the sinks and cabinets. Soaking a rag in teak oil, he polishes all the joiner work in the main cabin until the honey-colored woods glow in the sunlight streaming through the portlights. He takes satisfaction in the quality of the cabinetry joiner work, the care with which he built the interior of the boat from properly aged teak and mahogany and spruce.

Sorting clothes in the hanging lockers, he rearranges everything into a semblance of order. He even removes the floorboards that cover the bilge, sponges out the bit of water there, and wipes the bilge with a pleasant-smelling cleaner.

It takes several hours, but, when he's finished, the interior of the ketch is clean, organized, and presentable. He looks around one final time, then goes out through the main hatch and pulls his bosuns chair from the port cockpit locker and clips it to the end of the spinnaker halyard.

Then he wipes down the cockpit seats, the steering station and cabin top. Finally, he pulls a soft cloth along the teak cap rail that runs around the boat. Looking across the water at her house and garden and not finding her, he hopes she hasn't changed her mind about coming out to *Shearwater*.

Satisfied he's done all he can for the ketch, he pats Orion's haunches and goes below to change into fresh clothes.

When he comes back out to the cockpit and glances toward the house, he still sees no sign of Charlotte. He goes forward, stretches out on the cabin top under the warm sun, and thinks about his reluctance to share with her what happened to him in the war. How it started on a Sunday afternoon when the radio announced the attack on Pearl Harbor, while he and Djanette were having a late lunch in their apartment in Boston.

They had slept until late morning, and even all these years later, he can recall her sitting in her pink robe. For no special reason he'd bought her roses the day before, and she'd arranged them in a yellow vase on the dining table. They were listening to an NFL game when NBC interrupted the broadcast with news of the attack. He remembers her face turning ashen. Members of her family were still in Europe. From the day Hitler invaded Poland, she'd tracked the war in Europe. She understood immediately what the attack in Hawaii meant for America and its young men.

When he told her that he would have to enlist, she argued with him, begging him not to become involved. He recalls holding her, until she stopped pushing him away. After that day, everything changed.

Even before he could enlist, a recruiter from the Melville Training Camp in Rhode Island found him in Boston. They were looking for men who were candidates for officer training at Melville. The recruiters wanted intelligent, fit young men who would do well skippering the new PT boats, high speed, maneuverable craft that were heavily armed. Men who would not be afraid to come to close grips with the enemy and who already had experience on the ocean, under either sail or power.

At Melville, he learned how to drive the incredible PT boats on his home waters of Narragansett Bay. He'd never seen anything like those boats. So fast they created rooster tails at speeds up to forty-five miles an hour, and so physically demanding to operate, the men around him said PT stood for Plenty Tough.

When his training completed, he was selected to skipper a PT boat in the Pacific theater. John Kennedy was also chosen as a skipper in the same PT group. It seemed the additional years of maturity he and Kennedy had over the younger men pulled out of the colleges was one reason they were selected to be officers. Maybe the year he'd spent in Madrid, near the fighting in the Spanish Civil War, was another reason he was chosen as a leader. Few young men his age had seen war and death close at hand, the way he had.

He said a final goodbye to Djanette in a cheap motel just off the base. He understood that with her Armenian family history, and her own escape from Europe as a refugee, nothing he said could lift her fatalism. Or diminish her dread that she'd never see him again. All he could do was swear his love for her and voice his conviction he would return to her alive.

In November 1942, in the middle of a snowstorm, his squadron left Boston and traveled by train across country to San Diego, to be loaded on transport ships and shipped first to Hawaii and then to Corregidor. He saw just enough of the swaying palms, white sand beaches and balmy temperatures in San Diego in November to know he wanted to bring Djanette there some day, after the war.

Arriving in the Philippines, he and his co-skipper, Robert Sweeney, were given PT boat No. 138 and began running night missions with orders to sink any enemy vessels that moved through those waters. It wasn't long before they were in their first battle and had sunk a ship towing barges of ammunition and supplies. Sweeney was a big, rangy lad from North Carolina, with an infectious laugh and a congenial personality. In the small confines of the PT boat's bridge, and with the danger they shared on these night missions, he and Bob Sweeney bonded like brothers.

He had taken his father's advice and gone into the Navy rather than the Army, but he wasn't spared the scenes his father had wanted him to avoid. Being on a PT boat was completely different from serving on a destroyer. Or any of the other Navy ships that stood off at distances of miles and never saw the destruction their shells were causing on enemy ships.

A PT boat was more like close combat, especially using machine guns or torpedoes at close range. What he saw in the Pacific haunted his nightmares in the same way his father must have been haunted by what he'd experienced in the killing fields of France. Perhaps what his father saw was even more terrible, but Michael would never know for sure, because for the rest of his life, his father would never talk about what happened to him in that First World War.

In the Philippines and Solomon Islands, enemy destroyers were armed, fast and dangerous, and if they found his boat, he and his men could be blown out of the water with a single shell. Their only defenses were speed, maneuverability, and the smoke they could release from the stern in great billows that could hide them long enough to allow escape. Their biggest vulnerability was the flash that occurred each time they expelled a torpedo from the tubes mounted on the bow. If a destroyer crew saw this flash in the dark night, they immediately had a fix on the PT boat and would pound away with their big guns.

One night on a mission near a group of small islands, a destroyer saw the flash from their torpedo launch and gave chase. Even putting out a large smoke cloud and zigzagging over the ocean, their PT boat caught bullets from the machine guns on the destroyer. One of those bullets grazed his shoulder. Back at the base, the doctor told him he was grounded for at least a week. He argued vehemently with the doctor until the grounding order was lifted, leaving it to him to decide whether he would go on any missions in that week. But persuading that Navy doctor to lift the battle restriction would lead to the biggest regret of his life, leaving him with a burden of guilt and shame he hid from everyone.

Now he sits up on the cabin trunk looking across the water and wondering if Charlotte has changed her mind about visiting *Shearwater*. He sees dozens of seagulls roosting on the beach below her house, with more resting on her floating dock and on top of its tall pilings. Then, beyond the roosting gulls, he spots her coming down the path toward the dock ramp, and he pushes these painful Navy remembrances far from his mind.

Charlotte

She starts the outboard, waits for the engine to settle into a steady hum and then unties the bow and stern lines. As the skiff pulls away from the dock, she feels a stab of nervousness. She has only a vague idea of what to expect on his sailboat. And they'll be alone together in an intimate space, arousing anxiety but also excitement. She increases the throttle.

Pointing the skiff towards the anchored ketch, she ponders the question, *what if Ben learns she's visited Michael Cordero's boat?* A fellow fisherman could motor by the entrance to Eagle Cove and see her skiff tied up to *Shearwater*? It hadn't taken long after she arrived on Cambria Island to learn that gossip among the fishermen and their wives traveled at something approaching the speed of light.

If someone did see her skiff, she can imagine the conversation between Ben and the other fisherman the next time they rafted their trawlers together, breaking out cans of beer and sharing the latest news.

"Saw Charlotte's skiff tied up to a big sailboat in the middle of your cove, Ben, while you were away with Tommy. Can't imagine how in hell that rag topper got over the reef with a honkin deep keel."

"What do you suppose she was doing out there with that sailor," someone might chime in.

"Anyone know anything about who that rag topper was, and why he was in there?" Ben would ask.

And then as soon as this news got back to the wives, certain of them would pick up right where their husbands left off. More than likely, they'd be seated around Georgina Powell's dining table, drinking one cup of coffee after another until the pot was empty and a new one had to be made.

"Anything could have happened out on that sailboat between Charlotte and that sailor," one of them might say to start the conversation.

"She's never been one of us. Still some San Francisco in her. Have you seen that crazy painting in her living room?"

As the skiff plows over the water, it rousts a dozen floating gulls, and they launch into the air squawking in protest. In her head, over the hum of the outboard, Charlotte can hear the imagined conversation take a darker turn.

"I wouldn't put it past her to have done something with that sailor she shouldn't have."

"She's never been in love with Ben the way I love Gordy, I can tell you that."

"You know the old saying girls, when the cat's away…."

"Our Ben doesn't deserve that."

"The man works hard. Provides for his family."

She shakes her head and throttles back the outboard, but she can't stop the conversation running through her mind. After this many years with them, she knows how those women think.

"Ben is great with Tommy," she can hear one of them saying.

"Teaches him what a man needs to know. Can you imagine, Charlotte has Tommy reading poetry."

"Ben goes along to keep peace in the house."

"I think he's afraid she'll leave him," someone might chime in. "That he didn't deserve a woman like her."

She pushes the tiller over, and the skiff turns away from a log floating just below the surface. Her eyes are sharp, and she's accustomed to searching the water for deadheads like this one. She brings the bow back on course toward the ketch and increases the throttle.

Running her mind back over this imaginary conversation her reaction is *guilty as charged*, at least about Tommy. She's encouraged her son to appreciate art and poetry, and she's made his reading lists broader and more varied than the simple books most island parents give to their home-schooled children. And she's urged him to travel when he grows up. Some of the islanders haven't been much more than a hundred miles in any direction. In her presence at least, they've rarely talked about Europe or Asia, let alone the exotic places Michael mentioned over dinner.

I'm not going to worry about the possibility someone will see me out here, she tells herself, as the skiff slows. *I made a commitment to help Michael, and I intend to keep it.*

She cuts the outboard, and, when *Shearwater*'s gleaming white hull rears above her, she reaches up and grabs the gunnel. A boarding ladder drapes over the side, its bottom step almost touching the water. She pulls the skiff over to it. Orion's head appears above the lowest lifeline, his pale blue eyes gazing down at her, his tail beating hard. "Hello, Orion," she greets him.

"Permission to board," she calls in a loud voice. She's learned this much etiquette hanging around Ben's fisherman friends. You don't just step onto someone's boat for the first time without alerting them.

Grasping one of *Shearwater*'s stanchions, she stands up in the bottom of the skiff and ties off her bow line with two half hitches and then reaches down and kills the outboard.

The main hatch slides back and Michael emerges, his face breaking into a welcoming grin. "Permission granted."

He stands in the companionway, silhouetted by the sun. He's in sailing shorts and a simple T-shirt. She notices he's made another effort with his hair.

Before climbing the boarding ladder, she catches a hint of what he must have looked like in his twenties: his hair darker, his frame leaner. But he might not have been better looking then, she thinks. Men like Michael Cordero have a way of improving with age.

Michael

He emerges from the hatch and comes to the lifelines, reaching down for the carrots and asparagus she's brought from her garden.

"Some veggies for your larder," she says, handing them to him. She's wearing teal blue shorts and a white blouse, open at the throat, and boots.

He watches her nimbly clamber up the boarding ladder onto the deck, then stoop to rough Orion's thick fur, leaning her weight against his playful thrusts. That she's taken to Orion so readily deepens his attraction.

"Welcome to my home on the water," Michael says, when she rises. He places the vegetables on a cockpit seat and turns to her.

"This is beautiful," she says, gesturing around the boat.

You're beautiful is what he thinks.

"All these varnished woods," she says, "and the teak decks. Must be a lot of work."

"It takes some effort," he agrees. "But it's worth it."

The breeze blows strands of hair around her face. She brushes them back. "I can see that."

"Work first, or a boat tour?" he asks.

"Let's get your project done," she answers. "Then you can show me the boat."

"Would you mind taking your boots off?Black soles are a bit hard on the teak."

Her cheeks flush.

"I forgot to wear appropriate shoes," she says, sitting on the cabin top and removing her boots and socks. "I'm used to just grabbing garden shoes or boots. Doesn't make any difference on Ben's boat."

"I should have mentioned it last night," he says.

She begins to say something, as if she's about to comment on the evening they spent together. But then stops.

He waits, wondering what she'll say.

"Let's get on with the project," she says, finally.

He nods and leads her forward along a side deck. "Don't catch your toes on any of those," he says, pointing to the cleats mounted on deck, gleaming in the sunlight.

"The teak feels warm."

"The decks will be hot this afternoon," he says, stopping at the mast. He shows her a simple cloth seat. "This is my bosun's chair,"

She grins. "Looks like a playground swing."

He laughs. "It does. I'll sit in it, and together we'll crank me up the mast using the spinnaker halyard and this big winch." He points to the stainless-steel cylinder mounted on the mast. "I can take most of the strain off the halyard as I go up. At sea,

I use a block and tackle system to go up the mast by myself, if something goes really wrong up there."

"That can't be fun," she says.

"It's not," he agrees. "Especially in a big seaway." He cinches on his tool belt and turns to her. "Ready to try this?"

"Of course," she answers, but he detects a hint of tension.

"You can winch me up the first few feet," he says, "and we'll test it all out."

"What do I need to do?"

"You wrap this halyard around the winch three or four times like this," he says, showing her. "Always wrapping clockwise. Then you insert the winch handle."

"Let me try it," she tells him. "There were no winches on my dad's boat."

He watches as she grasps the rope and winds it around the winch and then clicks the handle in place.

"Perfect," he says. "You need to always keep tension on the halyard with your left hand, while you're cranking with your right."

"I can do that," she says.

They stand shoulder to shoulder at the mast.

"Once I'm up there, you wrap the loose end of the halyard around this cleat, crosswise like this," he says, demonstrating how to tie the rope off. "Everything stays that way until I'm ready to come down."

"Got it."

"Then we're set. On the way up, I'm going to want to stop at the spreaders," he says, pointing up the mast to two cross bars. "I need to inspect those and the spreader lights too."

"What are the lights for?"

"They illuminate the deck at night."

"So, I cleat you off when you're inspecting them?"

"You're a quick study," he tells her.

She grins.

He settles into the bosun's chair. "You'd make a good sailor."

"Let's see how I do while you're up there," she says, her face serious now.

"Up I go then."

Charlotte

She wraps the halyard tight around the winch, inserts the handle and begins cranking. It all feels new to her, and awkward. But there's something contagious about his confidence in her, and she watches as the bosun's chair rises, his tanned legs hanging suspended above her. With him pulling himself up the mast, it doesn't take her many rotations of the winch handle before he's hanging at the height of the spreaders. Then she ties the halyard off properly around the cleat.

"Well done," he calls down to her. "You can take a break. I'll be a few minutes at this position."

"How did your shoulder do?" she asks.

"Hardly felt anything," he answers.

As he hangs in the bosun's chair above her, she finds herself admiring his physicality, his resourcefulness. With all its lines, winches, and fittings, and the two masts and various sails, the ketch is complex. Yet his skill has allowed him to cross oceans in this self-contained world. Craning her neck to watch him work above her, she already feels there's some ephemeral quality about him when he's on this boat. *He's so fundamentally in his element.*

She sits on the cabin top, Orion lying at her feet and thinks back to when her father kept his tiny sloop on a side tie in the marina below Jack London Square. She'd had no idea what motivated her father to buy that sailboat. Perhaps he'd watched the white sails out on the Bay his whole life and longed to be among them.

One day, not long after buying the sloop, her father brought home a used book about sailing. They both studied the photos and all the labels on the boat illustrated in the book. They learned about port and starboard; tacks and jibes; the differences between sheets and halyards and stays; what the parts of a sail were: the luff, leech, foot, head, and clew. Now leaning back against Shearwater's mainmast, feeling the sun on her skin, she recalls most of that terminology. Her father's sailing book had explained that the names of a sailboat's parts were universal, used by sailors everywhere for centuries, allowing unambiguous communication between skipper and crew.

She can still remember that July day in 1928 when the wind was light coming through the Golden Gate Bridge. She and her father raised the sails for the first time, making the boat go to windward, just like the book had taught them, sailing away from the marina for half an hour, out toward the middle of the Bay. She saw gulls soaring and fish jumping, and of course other sailboats gliding along effortlessly, as they were.

When the wind became stronger, they jibed and brought the boat back towards the marina, running with the wind this time. She was not sure she'd ever seen her father happier than on that day. And she loved sharing it with him, just the two of them in the small space between the tiller and the mast, using their weight to balance the boat's heeling.

Fifteen months later, when the stock market crashed, her father lost everything, including the sailboat. She realizes now that thirty years have passed since she'd last stepped on a sailboat with him.

"I'm ready now," Michael calls down, pulling her out of these memories.

She uncleats the halyard and cranks him up the rest of the way to the top of the mast, beginning to feel comfortable with this responsibility, especially now that the nautical terms have come back to her.

"Another break?" she yells up.

"This will take longer," he calls down. "Make yourself comfortable. There's water and soft drinks in the galley if you're thirsty."

"I'm good" she tells him, arching her head back to watch him hanging in the bosun's chair forty feet above the deck.

"Be careful," she says, then feels her face flush, remembering he's done this, many times, and under much more difficult conditions.

"I will," he calls down, with no apparent annoyance.

With the halyard cleated off, she sits back down on the cabin top and continues to admire the beauty of his ketch. She takes in the varnished handrails, the curving strips of teak layering the deck, and the graceful flare of the cockpit. She's struck by the soft geometry of the boat, everywhere rounded corners, smooth-flowing lines. Are some men drawn to sailing craft like this one, she wonders, like they're drawn to the bodies of women?

The sun is warm, and she feels drowsy sitting on the cabin top. Her mind wanders back to sailing with her dad, how different his primitive boat had been, no varnished teak, no spinnaker, not even a cuddy cabin.

Lost in these memories, she absently pats Orion's flanks where he lies dozing on the warm teak deck when Michael calls down to her. "All finished up here."

She snaps out of her reverie and looks up. "Ready to come down?"

"Yes, nice and slow, please."

She moves to the mast, uncleats the halyard and begins unwrapping the line. But with only one wrap left around the winch, she misjudges the force of his weight and the rope rushes through her fingers as he drops ten or fifteen feet in a free fall.

"Whoa!" he shouts, just as she manages to tighten the halyard around the winch and arrest his fall. Her heart beats wildly at the thought he could have smashed into the deck and been injured, or even killed.

Michael

Even before his feet touch the deck, Charlotte is apologizing, her face flushed.

"It was my fault," he tells her, trying to ease her concern. "I should have told you to leave some wraps around the winch."

"You could have been seriously injured," she says, her green eyes still wide.

He shakes his head. "You did well. I was just surprised."

"I'll do better next time," she says in a determined voice.

That there might be a next time encourages him. "I appreciate your help," he says, putting a hand on the mast to steady himself as he steps out of the bosun's chair. "The rig is okay, and that's what matters."

"What about the small mast?" she asks, pointing to the shorter pole standing in front of the cockpit, its boom extending out to the transom.

"I checked the mizzen mast earlier," he tells her. "It's short enough I could do that alone."

"According to our home dictionary, two masts are what make this boat a ketch," she says.

"Yes," he answers, impressed she was interested enough to look that up.

"Why did you choose a ketch design?" she asks, standing next to him on the cabin top.

"With the sails split between two masts," he says, "each sail is small enough to handle by yourself in a blow. Important for single-handed sailing."

She looks at him, her face reflecting sunlight. "What sail plan would you choose if you had two aboard?"

His heart skips a beat. He thinks about her question while running a hand through his hair. "I'd probably choose a sloop. Simpler, with only one mast. If I had someone with me, we could handle the bigger sails, working together."

He searches her face, waiting to see if she has more questions. But his answer appears to satisfy her. "Let's take a break," he says, removing his tool belt. "I'll show you the boat. But first I want to show you what I saw from up the mast."

She moves with him to the railing and together they lean over and peer into the clear water, all the way to the silent resting sea floor, strewn with eddies of dark sand. Pale, iridescent jellyfish of every size surround the boat—fabulous gauzy hemispheres, limpid and shimmering. They oscillate silently through the green depths.

"Astonishing," she says softly.

He nods.

She points to an enormous jellyfish, its vacuous body glowing bright orange, trailing a five-foot train of undulating yellow filaments as it pulsates past the ketch. "That's a Lion's mane jelly. You don't see those often," she says. "They're one of the largest jellies in the world."

He lets out a whistle.

"This happens every few years," she says. "Something to do with the water temperature. Most of the small ones are Moon jellies."

He sees her shiver, bumps rising on her bare arms as she watches the ballet of the jellies. He struggles against the urge to pull her to him.

After they admire the jellies for a few more minutes, he leads her aft to the cockpit. At the companionway he turns to her. "It's best to go down the steps backwards."

He follows her down the main hatch. "Can I get you something to drink," he offers. "I have water, beer, a few soft drinks."

"I'm good for now," she answers.

Gesturing with his right hand, he says, "This is the main cabin and the galley where I cook."

He moves to the gimballed three-burner stove, all white enamel, and pushes on it with one finger. "The stove swings, so it's always level at sea. No matter how bad the boat heels."

"This galley seems small for the size of the boat."

"It's safer at sea that way." He wraps a wide leather belt hanging next to the stove around his waist. "If you're in a big blow, you can strap yourself in while you're cooking."

"That's neat," she says with a smile.

From the galley, he points to a built-in table, facing backwards with a small seat. "The chart table, for navigation," he says. "And a good place to read at night."

He opens a folding door, revealing a double berth filling a low-ceilinged compartment that stretches to the stern. "The owner's cabin. Works best if you're short."

She laughs and follows him forward, down the narrow aisle.

He points to each side. "Port and starboard settees. They can be used as single berths." Ahead of her, he squeezes around the mast, which comes through the deck, to the keel.

She follows him, sliding around the wooden spar as he pulls back a folding door that divides the main cabin from the forward compartment. He gestures toward the sink and toilet on one side and the hanging locker opposite, then points forward to a raised platform filled with gear. "The V-berth. Sleeps two, but as you can see, I use it for storage."

Next to her, pressed into the small space of the forward cabin, he feels a growing awkwardness. If she weren't married, if there weren't a Ben and a Tommy, right about now he would ask her if it would be okay to kiss her. But he says nothing, and she retreats past the mast, back into the main cabin.

Charlotte

"It's cozy, and functional at the same time," she says, glancing around the main cabin.

He nods. "It's been a great home for me and Orion."

Everywhere she looks, there's teak and mahogany—varnished or oiled in rich honey colors. Handrails, cabinet doors, the center table, all lustrous and gleaming in the soft light of the boat's interior. Even the alternating yellow and brown strips of wood on the cabin floor glow.

From the forward bulkhead, light glints off the polished brass ship's clock and barometer. She runs a hand over the rich burgundy covers on the berth cushions. She's never imagined the interior of a boat could feel this warm and inviting and comfortable. Everything close to hand, yet with a spacious feeling, from the open layout of the galley and berths to the high flare of the cabin ceiling.

The tension she'd felt motoring out from the dock, and winching him up the mast, has dissipated now. She'd half expected odors of mildew and bilge water but inside *Shearwater* she detects only the scent of an unfamiliar spice and a trace of lemon oil.

She inhales these scents and finds underneath them the unmistakable masculine smell of Michael himself, the same scent she found on his skin and in his hair when she replaced his bandages. Here it is again, inside his boat.

"Your boat is striking," she says.

"I'm glad you like her."

She glances at the rows of books on the shelves behind the berths. A notebook on the chart table labeled *Ship's Log* attracts her eye. She wonders if it recounts all the places he's sailed to, the adventures he's had.

"Do you have any other projects that need doing?" she asks.

He doesn't answer right away, and then shakes his head. "What I really want to do is try for Keller Peak again. I want to experience what makes it so special for you."

In the cabin's stillness, she hesitates, surprised he cares this much about her feelings for the mountain.

"If we take it easy this time," he continues, "especially on the steeper parts, I think I can make it to the summit."

"If that's really what you want to do," she says, still not understanding. "We can go more slowly on those steep parts. And you don't need to take a pack this time."

"That will help."

"But why so soon?" she asks. "What's the hurry?Why not recover more?"

His face becomes serious. "I looked at the tide tables again last night," he says in a soft voice. "I have only three more days here, Charlotte."

Three days.

"I need the highest tide of the month to take *Shearwater* over the reef at your entrance without risking damage to her keel," he explains. "And that tide comes on the afternoon of the fifth."

There's a dull roar in her ears as she focuses on what he's saying.

"The closer the fifth gets, the busier I'll be preparing to depart. This afternoon is the best time to try for the summit."

He's leaving in three days echoes through her mind.

In the last twenty-four hours, she's imagined what it might be like to have a life with him. Now, knowing he'll leave Eagle Cove in a few days, and that she'll never see him again, frightens her.

It creates within her something close to panic.

Michael

The entire time they hike the narrow trail up Keller Peak, mostly single file, he wonders what Charlotte is thinking. On *Shearwater*, when he'd told her he was leaving in three days, emotion had flooded her face. Yet she'd said nothing in response. Instead, she grew quiet. Then told him she had things to do before they went to the trailhead and left in her skiff.

Her silence as she hikes behind him, letting him set the pace this time, gnaws at him. *What did you expect?* he thinks, as they move between towering cedars and armies of sword ferns that line the trail. *Did you think she'd beg you to take her with you?*

The trail is laced with rocks and tree roots that are easy to trip over. He must be careful where he steps. Fingers of overgrown salal grab at his legs, slowing him further. He can't help feeling that somehow the mountain has turned against him, sensing his desire to take Charlotte away. But then he tells himself he's imagining things.

More than an hour of excruciating silence passes as he labors up the trail. At last, he breaks out of the trees onto the craggy rock pinnacle forming the summit, filled with relief he made it to the top only seven days after his injury. From here, the view is stunning in all directions. Below lies the sea's great expanse dotted with other islands, green smudges in the distance. Low on the eastern horizon stand the mainland's white-capped mountains. The sky above is a vast blue bowl, except to the north where dark clouds mass on the horizon.

"An incredible view," he tells her as she comes up beside him, Orion trotting next to her.

"Always," she agrees.

"Is that what draws you?" he asks, continuing to look at the sea and the distant mainland.

She doesn't answer right away, and he senses a growing tension.

"It's more than that," she says finally. "It's the place I came to for solace, after I arrived on the island."

He waits to see if she'll say more.

"This peak offers me more peace than anywhere else on the island," she continues. "Even the hideaway I showed you yesterday."

Still, he waits.

"I feel free up here," she adds. "Freer than anywhere I've been."

When it's clear she won't elaborate further, he searches for the right words. "Could you feel that way out on the ocean?" he asks.

For a long moment, she doesn't look at him. Over her shoulder he sees the dark clouds in the north pressing towards them. A sudden sharp gust of wind buffets them, and the temperature drops several degrees.

When she finally turns to him, she still says nothing, her green eyes filled with emotions he can't read.

Another wind gust hits them, stronger this time, and the clouds begin to block out the sun. He feels his chest constricting as the moments tick by. *Why won't she answer?*

She pulls in a deep breath and shudders, then reaches with one hand and strokes his face.

In the distance, a peal of thunder rolls towards them. Clouds shadow the summit now, sudden gusts pulling at their clothing.

Dizzy with feeling, he leans toward her. She raises her face, and he sees an eagerness in her eyes before she closes them. He kisses her, a tender, lingering kiss. Her hand caresses his neck and moves through his hair as she returns his kiss, her other arm coming around his back, pulling him to her.

He has her answer.

That's what he wants to believe as he lifts her off her feet and spins her around on the summit of Keller Peak.

Charlotte

His mouth is sweet, delicious. Her body melts into his, her breasts pressed against his chest. Finally, she can run her fingers through his hair and know with certainty what it's like.

She can smell rain coming and, opening her eyes, she sees the billowing black clouds in the north rushing down on them. But she doesn't care. Their breaths are ragged now. She feels him fumble with the buttons on her shirt. She helps him, and when her breasts come free, he bends his mouth to them, causing flutters in her belly. She puts both hands through his hair, arches her head back and feels sensation bloom inside her.

Just as he kisses her mouth again, with great need and urgency, a tremendous clap of thunder bursts over the mountain, echoing off the rocks around them.

"Now that's a kiss," she says, laughing.

He laughs with her. "Let's try it again," he says, pulling her to him.

Another kiss, and another burst of thunder. "It works," she shouts, laughing again.

But then lightning strikes, painting the peak stark white, splitting in half a lone cedar below them, with a sound like cannon fire. Tree branches explode and the trunk catches fire, flames rising into the first drops of rain. The thunder that follows is deafening.

She's not particularly religious but the lightning strike, just as she's kissing a man who's not her husband, suggests the heavens are angry, reproaching her for her lust. She tries to shake this superstition from her mind. But as the tree below them is consumed by fire, she's reminded of her childhood Sunday school lessons.

"We're the highest things on this mountain!" she shouts to him, above another peal of thunder rolling across the peak. "We need to get down, *now*!"

Overhead, quite abruptly, the entire sky is now dark. As the clouds above them open, she grabs his hand, and they scramble down the rock slab. "Orion let's go!" he yells to the Husky.

As they leave the rock and move onto the dirt path, heavy raindrops pound down, raising dust puffs. Then the clouds open. Within seconds, the trail becomes wet, the odor of rain-soaked duff rising to meet them.

In the trees, she stops to button on her blouse. "It's safer here."

"You look great soaking wet," he says.

She makes a face at him. "And your hair gets even crazier in the rain."

"Nothing a hot shower couldn't cure."

"We'll see about that," she says, "when we get to the house."

They run down the trail, drier now under the dense foliage. Orion races ahead of them, treating their descent as a game.

Even where the trail narrows, she feels Michael holding tightly to her hand, letting her slide ahead of him.

She feels expansive.

Her mind rushes down the mountain, to the house and the bedroom. She lengthens her stride, pulling Michael after her, running even faster.

Michael

He holds Charlotte's hand tightly as they race down the trail, careful not to let her stumble in the steeper sections. Wind gusts whip the tops of cedars and firs, and he hears rain pelting above them. But the dense forest canopy muffles periodic thunderclaps and shields them from the beating rain, making the sudden weather front seem less threatening.

When he thinks about what might happen between them at the house, the trail appears to go on forever. But finally, still holding hands, they burst out of the forest into the broad meadow and run side-by-side, breathless.

He glances at Charlotte. His heart races with more than their run's exertion. Together they take the porch steps two at a time, collapse on the bench, and pull off their muddy boots, their fingers fumbling with haste.

"The weather changes fast here," he says, rising from the bench and leaning over—hands on his knees—pulling in deep breaths. From the porch he can look out at the green forest, cedars and firs swaying in the wind, the scent of damp grass carried towards them from the meadow.

"The rule is wait ten minutes, and it'll be different," she says, in her stocking feet.

Recovering his breath, he reaches for her, the way he did on the peak. She comes to him willingly, pulling his wet t-shirt over his head and flinging it towards the porch bench. He begins to unbutton her blouse, and she helps him, all the while kissing him. They stumble through the front door into the living room.

Lightning turns the room white. Seconds later, thunder crashes above the house, leaving in its wake heavier rain, drumbeating on the roof.

She takes his hand, pulling him toward the stairs when, loud and shrill, the kitchen phone rings. They stop at the foot of the stairway, a frozen tableau, her hand grasping the banister.

She swivels to look at the phone, then back to him, hesitating.

He squeezes her hand. "They'll call back."

But as the phone continues to ring, she stares at it. This time when she turns to him her forehead is furrowed, her eyes filled with concern.

Charlotte

Standing in her bra in the living room, Michael bare-chested next to her, she counts the rings. *Four or five…that's a casual call, perhaps one of her friends wanting to talk about the thunderstorm.*

But the ringing continues. She grows anxious. Even as Michael's eyes beg her not to answer.

Seven…eight…nine…It's Tommy or Ben. She exhales the breath she's been holding and releases Michael's hand. Crossing the living room in three long strides, she picks up the phone with one hand while covering her chest with the other.

She sees Michael grab the windbreaker he left on the couch before their hike and follow her into the kitchen. He leans against the sink counter, leaving a discreet distance between them.

"How are you, sweetheart?" she asks into the handset.

She turns to Michael and mouths, "*Tommy.*"

"Dad and I are having a great time," her son tells her.

Michael pulls on his windbreaker and zips it up around his bare torso.

"That's wonderful," she says into the phone.

She feels Michael place a blanket around her shoulders, covering her. It's the Afghan from the side couch. She feels a surge of gratitude toward him. Now he goes out the front door and comes back in with her blouse and lays it on the kitchen counter next to her. She covers the mouthpiece, and he whispers, "You need privacy. I'm going."

She nods her thanks, turning back to her son's animated voice.

"Guess what, Mom, I caught a thirty-pound salmon!"

"That's terrific," she says, clamping the phone between her ear and her left shoulder as she pulls her blouse on. "I'm glad you're having a good time."

"We've seen seven bears so far. Big ones. Right on shore near us."

"That sounds exciting," she says, buttoning her blouse.

"The bears were fishing for salmon too."

"They're pretty darn good at that, aren't they?" She carries the phone, and its unwinding cord over to the wood stove, places three small logs inside, stuffs wadded paper underneath, and lights it, while cradling the phone to her ear.

"Are you doing something, Mom?"

"I'm just building a fire," she says, closing the stove door and latching it.

"We might be coming home early, Mom."

"Oh?" Her free hand flies up to her mouth.

"Yeah."

She glances through the kitchen window. Michael and Orion are starting down the path.

"Dad wants to talk to you."

Her throat thickens, and she has trouble finding her voice.

"You still there, Mom?"

"I'm here, honey. Please put your dad on, and congratulations again on that huge salmon."

"Thanks. Here's Dad."

"Hi Hon," Ben greets her. "How are things at home?"

"There's a thunderstorm here," she answers, trying to keep her voice even. "But everything's fine."

"I can hear the thunder through the phone," he says.

She can already feel the woodstove's heat. "How's your trip going?"

"Tommy's enjoying it, and so am I. We've got a lot of salmon iced in the hold."

"He's excited about that thirty pounder he caught," she says, trapping the phone between her ear and shoulder again, placing both hands over the stovetop. "It's the biggest fish he's ever landed," he says. "We're both looking forward to all the salmon dinners you can make from our haul."

"Sounds like I'll be busy when you get here," she says.

"Look, I'm calling to warn you there's a huge storm headed your way. A bad norther."

She takes the phone in her hand. "How bad?" she asks, unease in her stomach.

"One of the worst in years. We're already seeing some crazy winds up here, and the rain is horizontal."

"This thunderstorm must be the leading edge of it," she says. An image of herself and Michael half-naked in the living room flashes through her mind and her face grows warm.

"You're sure that same storm is coming south?" she presses him.

"Definitely. The forecasts say it will build as it heads your way. Sixty to seventy miles an hour, with heavier gusts."

"That bad?" she asks, her unease growing.

"Afraid so. Could be like the '49 storm."

She intakes a sharp breath. "We lost a thousand trees on the island then."

"I know. The dock washed out. Tommy was terrified."

She thinks about *Shearwater* being trapped in the cove.

"You have only a few hours to get ready," Ben tells her. "Make sure all the windows are sealed, and the skiff is double tied to the dock."

"I can do that. Are you and Tommy safe?"

"We'll find a secure harbor around Bella Bella. If not, we'll run all the way up to Prince Rupert. Don't worry about us."

"Tommy said something about coming back early."

"I think we're both ready to come home. As soon as the storm is over, we'll head south. If we push it, we should be back in three or four days."

She steadies herself against the wall.

"Make sure you bring in lots of firewood before the storm hits," he tells her. "And stay safe."

"I will," she assures him. "Take care of yourself and Tommy."

"Love you," he says.

"Love you too."

Hanging up, she grabs a hooded rain jacket from the hall closet and scrambles into it.

Yesterday, from the clouds and wind direction, she'd sensed a storm was coming. But concentrating so much of her time and attention on Michael, she'd stopped thinking about the weather.

She rushes out onto the porch and pulls on her boots. The rain is lighter now and down at the dock, Michael and Orion are climbing into the inflatable.

She runs down the path, shouting Michael's name.

Michael

He's settled into the inflatable, grasping the oars, when he hears his name. Faint, almost carried away by the wind. He glances at the house and sees Charlotte running down the path, waving both arms.

A lightning bolt flashes across the meadow, followed by rumbling thunder. Orion hunches down on the dinghy's floorboards, and Michael reaches over and pats the Husky's head. "It's all right, boy."

Along the beach, gulls stand motionless on the sand, like gray and white stones, the wind already too much for them. Behind the driftwood berm, madronas sway in the gusts.

The tide is low. He sees Charlotte hanging onto both railings as she comes down the steep dock ramp. *Was he too quick to leave her house?*

She stands over him as he sits in the dinghy. "Ben says there's a huge storm on the way," she tells him in a ragged voice. Her face is drawn and flushed at the same time.

This isn't what he expected, and a vague sense of alarm comes over him. "I didn't like the reading on my barometer this morning," he says, "but my radio is broken."

The air around them reeks of ozone and dripping moss. Dark clouds press down on the cove bringing a premature dusk. The herons and egrets that usually forage in the shallows are gone now.

She points north. "Ben says it's the worst storm system we've seen here in at least nine years."

He swears under his breath.

The wind blows her hair around her face, and she pulls it all back with one hand, continuing to avoid his gaze.

"Did he say how big the winds will be?"

"Sixty to seventy," she says without hesitation. "Gusting higher."

"Hell! That's of a lot of wind."

"In the '49 storm, we saw winds that high," she tells him, finally meeting his gaze. "Before the spinner on the barn broke off."

His mind rushes out to *Shearwater*. "What direction will the wind come from in the cove?"

She points across the water, already dotted with small whitecaps. "If it's like last time, straight through the entrance."

A hollow knot of fear balloons in his chest. "I need to get to my boat."

She gestures towards the house. "You and Orion can stay with me."

He feels himself hesitate, torn. "That's generous," he says, tempted for an instant by what her offer implies. *He could be with her, and it wouldn't matter how bad the storm was.*

She looks at him expectantly.

The inflatable rises and falls on the growing swells as the silence between them stretches. He's aware of the sharp creosote odor from the dock pilings and how fast the temperature is dropping, the wind gusts becoming more frequent.

"I appreciate your offer," he says finally. "But I need to be on *Shearwater*."

Through the drizzle, he sees reproach in her eyes. "That's crazy," she snaps. "There's nothing you can do for your boat. Not with winds that strong. The waves will build to five or six feet. In the shallow parts of the cove, they could be breaking."

"I understand," he says, trying to keep the edge out of his voice. "But I have to try."

Her mouth tightens. "I could see this morning how much you love *Shearwater*, Michael. But isn't your life worth more than the boat?" She lets the question hang in the air, then continues before he can respond. "At this time of year, survival time in the water is twenty or thirty minutes, before hypothermia kills you."

Sitting in the inflatable, he hesitates, glancing at Orion, then up at Charlotte, her auburn hair striking against her blue rain jacket. He shakes his head. "I can't just stay in your house and watch my ketch be destroyed. It's been my life, Charlotte."

Her eyes narrow. "Don't you think you should stop living in the past, Michael?"

He's too stunned to answer.

The atmosphere flares white again, the trees along the shore backlit by the stark illumination of another lightning strike.

"You don't seem qualified to give that advice," he says, recovering from the sting of her accusation. "What are you doing out here on Cambria except hiding from your past?"

As soon as he says these words, he regrets them. *You had no right to say that to her*.

He sees their impact register on her face as she stands open-mouthed.

He climbs out of the dinghy onto the dock and takes her arms in his hands, steadying them both. "I'm sorry I said that Charlotte, it was uncalled for. But I need to prepare *Shearwater* to ride out the storm."

Her eyes hold a challenge. "What can you do to make that possible?" she asks.

"If I weren't stuck in here, I could make a run for it. The safest place in a storm is at sea, as far from any lee shore as you can get. But since I'm trapped in here, I'll have to make the best of it."

"How?" she presses him. "What will you do?"

He shades his eyes and looks out at the water. "I can put out a second anchor, for one thing," he answers, turning back to her. "And I can take off the sails to reduce windage."

She takes a step back and he releases her arms. "Why can't you do that and then stay with me in the house?" she asks. "Where you'll be safe?"

"Because the most important thing I can do is run the engine, taking the strain off the anchor lines," he tells her. "Until the storm peak passes." He waits to let this sink in. "That's really my best hope…maybe my only hope…of keeping her off the rocks."

"Then for God's sake, let me help you!" she shouts above rumbling thunder, her eyes flashing. "You can't stay awake all night and then all day tomorrow."

"I'll have to try," he says. "There's no point risking both of us." He turns, ready to climb down into the dinghy. "I have to go."

Her face fills with frustration. He thinks she might hit him.

"Can't you see, it's the same for me now," she says in a tone that makes him feel as if he's failed to understand something important. Something obvious. "I won't be able to just sit in my house when you're out on *Shearwater*. I couldn't stand it!"

"What are you saying, Charlotte?"

"That I care deeply about you!" she says with sudden vehemence. She steps forward and grabs onto him as the dock rolls underneath them. "I don't know how it's happened in such a short time," she says in a disbelieving voice. "But there it is."

Another thunderclap, and a wind gust makes her hair fly again.

He's stunned into silence by her admission.

"Did you hear me, Michael Cordero?" she shouts. "I won't let you face the storm by yourself!"

Charlotte

She sees understanding dawn in his eyes and then on his face, as he pulls her into his arms. Now she doesn't care about the storm that's coming. She wants him to hold her, wants to feel his strength, his warmth.

His mouth is close to her ear, and he whispers, "I've been searching for you all these years."

A wind gust buffets them, and she leans into his embrace. "This is a hell of a time and place for revelations like this," she says.

"I didn't know how to tell you."

Another lightning flash, but this time she doesn't think about the burning tree on Keller Peak. For now, she's willing to allow herself the freedom to not worry about consequences or repercussions. An immense need burns inside her to be with this man, on his boat in this storm. Whatever that brings.

"I have to get the boat ready," he says, releasing her.

"And I have things to do for the house before I can join you."

"You're sure you want to do this, Charlotte?"

She feels herself glaring at him. "What if the situation were reversed? Would you let me go on the boat and risk everything alone?"

"No, of course not."

"Then let's stop wasting time."

"Okay," he says, "I'll come back for you."

She waves him off. "I can come out in my skiff."

The wind continues to pipe up and peals of thunder roll above them.

He shakes his head. "Your skiff won't make it through the storm tied to *Shearwater*. My inflatable can be brought aboard and lashed down on the foredeck."

"Okay. I'll be waiting here in ninety minutes."

"Bring your best foul weather gear. And warm spare clothes."

"What about Orion?" she asks, pointing at the Husky, hunched in the bottom of the dinghy.

"He hates this kind of storm."

"He could stay in the shop. It has a dog door that opens to the covered and fenced run Ben built for the retriever he had as a teenager."

"Then take Orion with you. He'll go…he doesn't want to be out in this."

"I'll leave plenty of food and water for him in the shop and the run. And for Toby in the house."

"While you're doing that, please leave the lights on in an upstairs room facing the water."

"Why?"

"Once it's dark, we'll need a reference point," he says, "to tell whether the anchor is dragging."

"Then I'll leave the lights on in Tommy's room."

"Good."

She sees him glance at *Shearwater*, already rolling in the waves and straining at anchor.

"Are you sure you want to do this?" he asks again, as rain beats on the dock and the air sizzles with electricity. "There's so much risk involved."

She rises on her toes and kisses him. "Go!" she says. "I'll see you here in ninety minutes."

Michael

After working to get the boat ready, he comes on deck in full foul weather gear. Three-foot waves are marching across the cove, crashing on the driftwood-strewn beach in explosions of white spray. He glances at the instruments in the cockpit and sees the anemometer at the top of the mast reads 30-35 knots. This wind is making high-pitched music in the rigging while a loose halyard bangs against the mizzenmast like a drumbeat.

He lowers an empty five-gallon diesel fuel container into the bottom of the inflatable, climbs down the stern ladder and pulls the starter cord on the outboard. The engine catches, then dies. He yanks the cord again, harder. Nothing. He hasn't used the outboard in months, preferring the exercise of rowing, and he wonders if the little 5-horsepower motor will work at all. Over and over, he pulls the cord, cursing under his breath. *What if he can't get back to the dock?*

Finally, on the sixth pull, the outboard spits, coughs, and catches. He's been holding his breath. Now he lets out a sigh as the engine settles into a ragged hum.

He casts off, gives the outboard a little throttle and brings the dinghy out from behind the shelter of *Shearwater's* hull. Instantly, a windblast catches the inflatable, and it begins surfing towards shore, slewing from side to side on the waves. The cove's surface reflects a dark, threatening sky.

Approaching the dock, he executes a tight circle, brings the bow into the wind, and stops the dinghy's forward motion, allowing him to grab a cleat. The inflatable hugs the dock while he glances at his watch, then at the house. It's past their agreed time and still no sign of Charlotte. *Maybe she came to her senses and will stay in the house. Or maybe Ben called again.*

He's about to climb onto the dock when Charlotte bursts out the front door and off the porch. Despite his concern about putting her in danger, he's relieved to see her. Wants to be with her, whatever the circumstances.

She comes down the path wearing a yellow foul weather jacket with matching waterproof pants and a large duffle bag hung on a strap over her shoulder. Of course, she would have appropriate gear for bad weather, he thinks, given the time she spends on Ben's boat. The rain begins to fall harder now, blown sideways by the wind.

"The storm's really coming on now," he shouts to her as she comes across the rolling dock, grabbing a piling to keep her footing.

"It'll get a lot worse before it gets better," she responds, handing him the duffle bag.

"I made hot soup and coffee, and enough sandwiches to keep us going. Even with your gimballed stove, I thought it would be hard to make anything on board in the weather that's coming."

"Good thinking," he tells her. "I didn't have time to do anything about food or drink. But I managed to put out the second anchor, replace the mainsail with a storm sail, and mount the outboard on the dinghy."

"Sounds like a lot," she says.

"It's a start. How's Orion?"

"He came right with me. He'll be fine."

"Is that a diesel fuel tank?" he asks, pointing at the large cast iron tank, near the dock ramp.

She nods. "Two hundred gallons. The fuel barge just filled it last month."

"Would it be okay for me to take five gallons?"

"Of course."

"Thank you," he says, relieved. "No way to know how long we'll have to run the engine." He lifts the diesel container. "Be right back."

When he returns with a full jerry can, Charlotte is sitting in the bow.

He hands her a life vest. "This is a spare," he says. "We could have trouble getting out to the boat, against these waves."

He waits until she's secured the life vest, then casts off and guns the outboard, pointing into the wind. Immediately, spray booms over the inflatable's bow, soaking their foulies. He angles off twenty or thirty degrees, but with the two of them in the dinghy and the weight of the duffle and jerry can, the gunnels are only six inches above the water. Wave tops begin breaking over the gunnels, filling the inflatable with seawater.

"I need to bail!" he tells her. "Can you take the outboard?"

"I'll bail," she shouts into the wind, "it's better with your weight in the stern keeping the bow up." She grabs the yellow bucket and starts heaving water over the side.

He tries to get more power out of the outboard, but the throttle is wide open. *Hell, I've put her at risk before we've even made it out to Shearwater.* But as he watches her bailing water from the bottom of the inflatable, he's filled with respect for her willingness to help. He sees already she has a measure of physical courage—the kind needed to sail the world's oceans on a boat like *Shearwater*—and that realization excites him.

Gradually the dinghy claws its way across the cove, slamming against the waves, showering them with spray. Charlotte bails one full bucket after another until, at last, they're in *Shearwater's* lee, where they can reach up and grab the cap rail. Working together they pull the inflatable over to the transom ladder.

"You go first!" he shouts above the wind.

She bails a final bucket and scrambles up the ladder. He gives her the bow line and waits while she ties it to a cleat. Then she reaches down for the duffle and then the jerry can. She knows what needs to be done, he thinks, probably from experience on Ben's trawler.

He unclamps the outboard, stands up in the inflatable with it, and hands it up to her. "It's heavier than it looks."

"That diesel can wasn't light," she says, with a half-smile.

He joins her on deck amid wind already shrieking in the ketch's rigging. "I could use your help pulling the inflatable aboard," he tells her, leading the dinghy forward to the bow.

She follows him along the side deck and together they lean over the railing and heave the dinghy up to the lifelines. Suddenly, a stronger wind gust catches the inflatable and flings it up in the air like a giant rubber kite.

"Pull it down!" they shout in unison, wrestling the dinghy to the deck and laying their bodies across it. "This would be laughable if it wasn't so serious," he says, his face close to hers.

She turns to him. "I've always wanted to lay across an inflatable with a good-looking sailor on a boat's heaving deck."

He laughs, impressed by her gallows humor. "Tie downs are behind the chart table," he says. "Do you want me to get them?"

"I'll get them," she says, struggling to be heard above the howling wind and banging halyards. "I'm not sure my weight can hold this thing down."

He watches her scramble aft on her hands and knees. *Shearwater* bucks and rolls in the building waves as he lies across the inflatable, feeling the wind trying to lift it under him. When she brings the ties to him, he positions the dinghy on the foredeck and begins tying it down.

The wind's scream in the rigging is un-nerving now. "You can go below," he shouts. "I'll come down as soon as I finish lashing the dinghy."

He watches her until she's safely at the cockpit and then turns to his task, knowing he needs to make certain the inflatable is securely tied down, no matter how hard it blows.

Charlotte

Holding a lifeline in one hand, and the handrail on the cabin top in the other, she scrambles aft to the cockpit and then lowers herself backwards down the companionway as he had shown her that morning. *Could it really have been this morning that she came onto his ketch for the first time?* She flashes to their climb up Keller Peak, Ben's phone call, her declaration to Michael on the dock. So much has happened to change her life in the hours since she winched him up the mast.

She reaches out and grabs her duffle from where she left it on a cockpit seat and brings it below. Then she pulls the hatch closed, thankful for the relative quiet. The ketch's solid wood construction muffles the howling wind more than she would have predicted. Standing in the main cabin, holding onto a handrail that runs above her, she sees Michael has stowed everything that was loose when she toured the boat in the morning. And here, at the boat's center, the motion is not as violent as it was on the foredeck.

She takes off the life vest he'd given her and removes her foul weather jacket. Warmth is emanating from a kerosene heater mounted on the forward bulkhead, and she warms her hands there. Then she takes the sandwiches from the duffle and puts them in one of the coolers.

Michael pushes back the main hatch cover and comes down the companionway steps, closing the hatch behind him. "How are you doing?"

"I'm okay, but I just realized you don't have an inside steering station," she says, "like the one on Ben's trawler. I don't know why I missed that this morning."

He peels off his yellow foul weather jacket at the companionway and hangs it in the wet locker. "Most sailboats have to be steered from the cockpit," he tells her.

"That's going to be rough in this weather."

"There is a dodger," he says, sitting down at the chart table in his foul weather pants. "It provides some protection at the helm. Or you can stay below. I made up a berth," he says, pointing to the starboard settee. "We can take turns trying to rest or sleep on a watch system."

The boat shudders under a windblast. Through the portlights she sees the sky has darkened into dusk. Michael lights two kerosene lamps hanging from the curved ceiling above them, at both ends of the cabin.

"How do you want to stow the soup and coffee?" she asks him, removing the thermos bottles from the duffle.

"Let's put them in this compartment," he says, indicating a locker in the galley. "They'll be secure there no matter how violent the motion gets."

She puts away the thermoses and turns to him. "What do we do now?"

"I'm going to change into dry clothes," he tells her, pulling off his yellow foul weather pants. "I didn't have time to do that when I was putting out the spare anchor. And then we'll fire up the diesel and start taking the strain off the anchors."

While she sits on the port settee, he goes aft into the captain's cabin and doesn't bother to close the folding door. This is not a situation that calls for modesty, she tells herself. From where she sits, she catches glimpses of him in various state of undress as he peels off his wet clothes. The scar on his back is not as pronounced now.

When he comes out, he's wearing an oiled and braided wool sweater and heavy woolen pants. "It's important to stay warm and dry tonight," he says, "given what we're going to face. I have spare clothes from when I sail in Alaska or the Southern Ocean. They'll be baggy but you're welcome to them."

"Let's see how I do with what I brought," she says. "The winters here are cold. I'm used to being on the water in a blow."

From the wet locker next to the companionway, he removes a different set of foul weather gear—heavier and red instead of yellow—along with high-topped sea boots. "We can use a watch system," he tells her, pulling on the water-proof pants and boots. "Four hours on, four off. Will that work for you?"

"I can do that."

"Good. When it's time, I'll take the first watch."

"Do you have enough fuel to run the engine all night?"

He nods. "We do now, with the extra five gallons. Enough until mid-day. Hopefully, the storm will blow out by then."

"I'm starting to feel queasy down here," she confesses to him. "Do you have any ginger ale aboard."

He opens a galley cooler and removes a can. "I always carry some."

She takes the can from him, feeling the warmth of his hand, wanting it to linger on hers. "Until I get used to this motion, I think the cockpit is better for me."

"You can wrap yourself in this and sit under the dodger," he says, offering her a heavy woolen blanket that looks like it was woven a long time ago.

"Thanks," she says taking it from him.

His face is soft in the glow from the kerosene lamps. He slides into his red foul weather jacket and zips it up to cover his mouth. With his nor'wester hat pulled low over his eyes, almost all his face is covered.

She puts on her foul weather jacket and follows him out into the cockpit, carrying the blanket and the ginger ale can. On the starboard cockpit seat, tucked under the dodger where the wind is blunted, she wraps the blanket tight around her body and watches Michael go to the wheel, reach down, and start the diesel. She can barely hear the engine over the howling wind, but through the seat cushion she can feel it thrumming under her.

The light is almost gone now but looking through a plastic window in the dodger, she can see waves crash over the entrance reef, sweep across the cove and smash onto the opposite beach in sprays of foam and spindrift. Anxiety runs through her, and she turns to look at Michael. At the wheel, he glances continuously at the instruments in front of him and then at the light coming from Tommy's window, reaching down every few minutes to adjust the throttle.

But now, as if he senses her, he looks up and gives her a broad, reassuring smile.

She knows it will be a long, wild night. But if they're together, she's ready to face it.

Michael

An hour later, it's completely dark. The only light outside the boat comes from Tommy's window on shore. The cove has disappeared. Their world has shrunk to the shrieking wind and the waves breaking around them with increasing force. He waits for a lull in the wind's hammering, leans over the wheel and asks her, "How are you feeling?"

From where she's huddled under the dodger, wrapped in the blanket he'd given her, she says, "Better. The ginger ale helped. I can go below now and have some soup."

"There are flat-bottomed bowls above the galley sink."

"I'll find what I need," she says, sliding back the hatch.

Thirty minutes later she comes out of the companionway carrying a thermos bottle. "You need some too," she tells him. "And here's a sandwich."

"Thanks," he says, gesturing to the wheel. "Can you take her for a few minutes?I can eat this, and you'll have some practice at what you'll need to do on your watch."

"Tell me what I need to know," she says, coming around the steering pedestal to stand next to him.

He reaches down to the engine throttle. "By matching the engine to the wind's strength, I try to keep the boat from being pushed backwards, putting strain on the anchor lines. But you don't want to give the engine too much power, because then the boat will move forward and pull the anchors out. As much as possible, we need to stay in a constant position."

"Let me try it," she says, trading places with him.

"You want to make small adjustments, like this," he says, showing her the appropriate range of motion. "The light in Tommy's window is your reference point."

"Got it," she says.

He sits under the dodger and spoons hot soup from the thermos, watching as she reaches down and adjusts the throttle to the wind strength, glancing at the light in Tommy's window from time to time. *She's competent, focused, and learns quickly*.

"That's it," he tells her. "You're doing well."

When he's finished, he reaches down through the companionway and puts the thermos bottle in the sink. Then he goes around the steering pedestal and places his mouth close to her ear. "Get some sleep now. Your watch will come all too soon."

"I'll try," she says, moving to the companionway. After lowering herself into the cabin, she pulls the hatch shut from inside.

He turns to look at the light from Tommy's window and judges the boat has held its position despite the increasing wind. Now he's confident that when it's his turn to go off watch, he can trust *Shearwater* to her.

He stands alone at the helm, the normal state of things on his voyages. Charlotte's presence on *Shearwater* fills him with determination to face the storm with all the strength and resources he can muster.

In the black night, he listens to the song of the standing rigging and hears the notes rising in pitch as the wind continues to build. He wonders what kind of song the rigging is singing, and what it might portend for them.

As the hours drag on and the boat's motion becomes more violent, he thinks about the ketch's thin skin, only half an inch of Maine cedar over oak frames. Sometimes when he's a thousand or two thousand miles out to sea, this same thought comes to him. A tissue paper-thin hull is all that separates him from the immensity of the sea below.

But then he must put this corrosive thought out of his mind, or he couldn't be a long-distance sailor. He's able to push such fears away in part because he built Shearwater himself, and he knows every plank, every frame, and every fitting in her.

In the darkest part of the night, riding the waves on *Shearwater's* hull, he thinks back to how he came to build her. When the war was over, the Navy returned him to the States through San Diego, where he was discharged. Desperate to see Djanette, he wasn't willing to take the train. Instead, he wangled a seat on a military transport from LA to Boston. He came back to an empty apartment and stood puzzled in the living room, until he found her note telling him she'd gone to New York to have surgery on her leg and would stay with her uncle's family, which he had visited with her before the war.

He didn't have a phone number for her uncle and caught the first train to New York City. He raced to the family's apartment building in the Bronx where her uncle ushered him into the apartment and said he should sit down. Then the uncle told him Djanette had died two months earlier, undergoing surgery to fix her deformed leg. That she had wanted to surprise him when he returned from the war. She'd no longer have the limp she'd had her whole life. But the operation had gone horribly wrong. When she went into cardiac arrest, they were not able to save her.

He sat on their living room couch in disbelief. Her uncle, and other members of her family, tried to console him but he was beyond consolation. They had had time to deal with her death. For him, it was as if those surgeons had cut out his heart. His beloved Djanette was gone.

Her family invited him to stay with them, but he declined. The life he'd dreamed of the entire time he was in the Pacific had vanished.

He went home to Newport to stay with his parents. When his mother saw him for the first time since he'd enlisted, she broke down and wept while holding him. His father's eyes filled with tears too. They were crying with happiness he'd come back from the Pacific alive but when he told them Djanette had died, they were heartsick.

For weeks afterwards, he drank himself into a stupor every night at a seedy bar down at the docks. When it closed at two in the morning, he'd stumble home a mile in the dark and the next day sleep into the afternoon before heading back to the bar.

His parents begged him to stop drinking and find something to do with his life. But he saw Djanette's death as a payback for what happened that August night in the Solomon Islands and felt he didn't deserve to live.

When it was almost too late, he realized he wouldn't survive to see another year. He sobered up long enough to decide he would build a sailboat and return to his youthful dream of seeing the world under sail.

He asked his father if he would design a forty-foot ketch capable of sailing anywhere in the world. Although his dad was in his eighties and retired by then, he designed a ketch of classic beauty, with long overhangs, a pronounced shear, and a low deckhouse. It was to be his final design, as he died a year later and never saw the completed boat.

After mourning his father, he searched for a yard where he could build the ketch. He knew the best wooden boat builders were in Maine and he had sailed that coast as a teenager. Now he returned there and arranged for space in a yard in Brooklin where he could build the ketch to his father's design, borrowing expertise and renting tools from the master builders around him.

It took most of his Navy pay and four years, living alone in a rented cabin in Brooklin, to finish the ketch. When the time came to christen her, he wanted to name her *Djanette*. But he realized he'd have to explain again and again what the name meant to him, and that would be far too painful. Instead, he named the ketch *Shearwater*. By the time he finished building the boat, he knew he would sail the vast reaches of the Pacific Ocean like those magnificent seabirds, traveling thousands of miles over the open sea without stopping, hoping to start a new life.

Charlotte

Deep in sleep, she dreams of shearwaters. Dozens of them, gliding over rolling blue water, their wingtips clipping white wave tops. In her dream, she's flying with them, soaring on the wind above the vast sea, free to fly as far as her wings will take her.

Through the blanket she feels someone's hand on her arm. Whoever it is, they're calling her name from a long distance, and the shearwaters are gone.

"Charlotte."

She tries to open her eyes.

"Wake up," a gentle voice urges her.

She remembers she's on *Shearwater*, in a storm, and now she's aware of the boat's violent motion. In the red glow from the chart table, she sees Michael sitting on the berth across from her, still in his foul weather gear. At some point he must have turned down the kerosene lamps, leaving the cabin mostly dark, letting her sleep.

She sits up on the settee and clears her head. "What time is it?" she asks him, holding onto the berth.

"Two forty."

"You were supposed to wake me at one."

"We have a long time to go. The wind isn't showing any signs of peaking, and the barometer is still dropping."

He holds out a steaming mug. "There's coffee if you want it," he says.

She takes it from him. "How are things outside?"

"Listen." He rises and cracks the main hatch open. She hears a tremendous roaring.

"I thought it might have lessened by now," she says, sipping the hot coffee.

He pulls the hatch closed. "It keeps building."

"I need to splash cold water on my face," she says, setting the coffee mug on the gimballed stove. "And I'll take you up on that offer of heavier clothes."

While he goes forward into the V-berth, she washes her face and uses the head. He comes back with a heavily cabled woolen sweater like the one he's been wearing, and woolen sweatpants. She puts them on and wrestles her foul weather gear over them.

"Your turn to sleep," she says, as they both hang on to overhead hand holds. The boat staggers now as each wave hits, and she wonders how she slept through the wild motion.

"I'll try, but first I need to raise a storm sail on the mizzen mast. It'll help steady the boat."

She follows him out into the cockpit and looks forward. Waves are breaking over the bow now, solid water pouring down the side decks, past the cockpit coamings.

He cups his hands around his mouth. "Can you take the throttle?"

"Got it," she shouts. The wind seems to have a heavy weight behind it now, pushing at her. She clutches the wheel tightly, to keep from being blown aft.

When he's finished with the mizzen sail, he asks, "Will you be okay if I go below?"

"I think so," she tells him. "I'm hoping dawn comes soon."

He glances at his watch. "Less than three hours. But find me if anything changes."

"I will."

"Wake me in four hours for my next watch."

"Go sleep," she tells him.

"I'll try." He steps close to her. "Charlotte…."

She looks up from the wheel. "What?"

"I'm grateful you're here."

"No place I'd rather be," she says, dryly.

He reaches across the wheel and kisses her.

"Go sleep!" she tells him again, in a voice that sounds like an order.

After he's gone below, the dark magnifies the wind's frightening roar, the incredible sounds the boat is making. Everything shaking or banging, unlike anything she's heard before. Around her, in the blackness, she hears waves breaking and hissing as they roll past.

An hour passes. And then another. She fights the boat's hypnotic roll.

Only after she's stood at the wheel for almost three hours, continually adjusting the throttle, does the faintest hint of dawn creep into the low cloud cover to the east. A new day arriving.

She turns toward the hidden dawn and begs it to come faster. Daylight will reveal the chaotic seas and bring its own anxiety. But anything is better, she tells herself, than listening to the wind scream in the boat's rigging in the black night, the hull groaning and creaking, as if the boat is coming apart. Darkness, and these terrorizing sounds, brought fear to her, and she doesn't need that. Doesn't want it.

Despite the extra woolen clothes Michael gave her, cold has seeped into her bones, making her shiver. The whole time she's been in the cockpit, the wind has kept building, the waves growing in height and power. Now the anemometer reads forty-five to fifty knots, with gusts to sixty, and the boat's motion has become even more violent.

Her neck is sore from glancing back at Tommy's window, adjusting the throttle to wind strength and waves. She thinks she's kept *Shearwater* in a relatively constant position, relieving the strain on the anchor lines, and soon it will be light enough to use other markers.

She has no intention of waking Michael after only four hours. The storm could carry on for another full day and night, and he needs his rest at least as much as she does.

As more light seeps into the menacing cloud cover above the island, she can see the wind's full effects. The cove's surface is a maelstrom now. Towering waves crash on the shore, driving the driftwood berm higher up the beach, toward the madronas. At the center of the bay, wave tops are sheared off by the wind and despite the protection offered by the dodger, she can taste salt in her mouth, feel it sting her eyes.

Along the shore, cedars and firs sway violently and she can see branches snap off and fly through the air. The sky is torn with flying scud and racing clouds. In the growing light, the water turns the color of slate, and for an instant, she thinks that color is something she could use in a painting. Then the violence of the boat's motion draws all her attention again.

Morning dawns grey and somber, with stinging horizontal rain, the wind even more gusty. Holding tight to the wheel and constantly adjusting the throttle in time with the gusts, she thinks about something Michael said to her on one of their walks along the beach. The biggest mistake is to believe the sea cares about you, he told her. Don't take its beauty for any kind of compassion. The sea is patient, he said, waiting for you to make an error in judgment or to become complacent. Remembering his words, she shivers again, and this time it's not from the cold.

She's been at the wheel for almost five hours when there's a loud bang from the bow, and the ketch begins to accelerate backwards. She rams the throttle forward and tries to hold position.

"Michael!" she screams as loudly as she can.

When he doesn't appear in the companionway, she scrambles around the wheel, pushes back the hatch, and screams his name again. She sees him stir in the berth and then sit up. He's been sleeping in his foul weather gear.

"Something's happened," she yells, "the boat is moving." She rushes back to the throttle and a moment later Michael climbs out into the cockpit.

"I think one of the anchor lines let go," she shouts. "Was it my fault?"

He shakes his head. "Amazing you've made it last this long."

She's reassured by the respect in his voice.

He points toward the bow. "Need to check the other anchor."

She grabs his arm and pulls him close. "I'm afraid of you going over the side. I'll never get you back aboard."

"I'll clip into the jack line," he says, pointing to a heavy rope running the boat's length on the port side. She watches as he pulls on a harness and tether and clips a shackle onto the rope.

"Be careful!"

He nods and crawls towards the bow on all fours. Moments later, he comes back to the cockpit and bends close to her. "Second line is almost chaffed through. Wrapped it as best I could. Not sure it will last long."

"What now?"

"Keep running the engine."

"How much fuel left?"

She watches him study the instruments under the port cockpit seat.

"There, four hours," he shouts above the wind's roar. He comes around behind the steering station and relieves her, but she remains close to him.

"Storm still hasn't peaked," she tells him.

"Getting worse. Barometer still dropping."

"What happens when fuel runs out?"

"There's a survival suit in the wet locker. I want you to put it on."

"We're in that much trouble?"

"A precaution."

"You'll put one on too?"

He looks away.

She waits, clutching his arm against the boat's shuddering motion.

He turns back to her with dismay in his eyes.

"There's only one suit aboard."

Michael

He sees her eyes widen and reaches for her hand. "There's another option," he says, leaning close so they can hear above the wind's roar. "You take the inflatable, with the wind behind you and ride the waves to the beach."

Sudden hope in her eyes now. She squeezes his fingers. "We both go."

He shakes his head. "Too much weight in the dinghy. We'd never make it. And I can't leave her, Charlotte."

She looks at him with a glinting fierceness in her green eyes. "Then I'm not leaving either. Not putting on your survival suit. We save *Shearwate*r together or . . . ."

"That makes no sense!" he shouts above the wind.

She glares at him. "I couldn't live with myself, using your survival suit."

He thinks about how quickly they've run out of options. Around them, waves heave and break as they roll past, hissing like snakes. He stares at the white crests breaking all over the cove and fights the hopelessness that's trying to undermine his resolve to save the ketch. Now it's come down to saving themselves as well.

He wants more than anything that no harm come to this woman standing next to him. Yet the storm is still growing, the wind rising, the waves incessantly pounding *Shearwater's* hull. He turns away from the horizontal rain pelting them and thinks this is the way it always happens when danger approaches. You make decisions and one of them is a miscalculation or a wrong assumption. The problems compound, until your options narrow, like a door closing behind you that can't be opened again.

These thoughts are broken by a terrifying screech from the bow roller.

"The second anchor's going!" she shouts.

He spins the wheel and jams the throttle forward. Slowly the ketch rounds into the wind and moves ahead and the screeching stops.

"What now?" she asks, searching his face, expecting answers from him.

"After fuel runs out, there's only one option left."

"What?"

"Sail her in the cove."

"Can we do that?"

"We'll have no choice."

Charlotte

She retreats under the dodger and motions for him to join her. "We should start sailing now," she tells him when he locks the wheel and comes around the steering station to stand next to her. "If we wait for the fuel to run out, we'll ruin the engine."

There's a momentary lull in the wind, as if it's pausing to mount another, larger attack.

But the lull gives them time to speak in more normal voices under the dodger's shelter.

"How do you know about that?" he asks her.

"From Ben. Never let tanks go dry."

"He's right. I was waiting to kill the engine until just before we run out."

"Then let's sail her now," she tells him. "She's a sailboat, isn't she? Why are you hesitating?"

He leans closer to her. "There's so little room in the cove. We'll be switching tacks constantly. Many hours. Maybe a full day. Maybe more."

"At least we'd have an anchor aboard when the storm ends."

He holds her gaze. "You're confident we're going to make it?"

"Aren't you?"

He looks at the massive waves rolling past them, and then back to her. "I have doubts," he confesses. "Not about the boat.

It's our endurance. Once we start sailing, we can't stop. No watches. No rest. Just the two of us continually wrestling with the wheel and grinding winches."

"Not a time for doubt," she tells him. "Why are you looking at me that way?"

"You amaze me," he says. "Your courage."

She doesn't tell him how much fear she felt in the dark night as the storm built. The boat's motion growing more violent, the wind's unnerving scream in the rigging, none of it familiar to her. No experience on the *Emerald Rose* has come close to the danger they're in now. Yet somehow, she's summoned resilience she didn't know she had. From the moment she made the decision to join him on the boat, she felt herself changing into someone new. Or maybe becoming the woman she's always been, but hasn't allowed herself to be, until now.

"Someone can speculate about what they *might* do," Michael is saying to her in the relative quiet under the dodger, "But you don't find that out about yourself until you're tested."

"This is a hell of a test," she tells him, drawing strength from his words.

He glances past her. "I'll raise the storm trysail. Then we can bring up the anchor."

The wind rises and falls in gusts, appearing to bide its time before striking with full force again.

"I'll signal you with my hands. Forward…steady throttle… back off," he says, making open hand gestures.

"Okay," she says.

"When I've brought in as much of the line as I can, you'll have to power forward to break out the anchor."

"Done that many times on *Emerald Rose,*" she assures him.

"Good," he says. "Once the anchor's aboard, I'll come aft, and we'll turn off the engine. How much do you remember from sailing with your dad?"

"We can't sail directly into the wind. Need to point off forty or so degrees on either side."

He nods. "The wind will try to drive the boat down the cove. Hopefully, she'll claw forward."

"How far do we go?"

"Until we run out of room. Then you put the wheel over, I release the sheet from the winch, the sails go across and I grind in on the other winch."

She says, "We sail in the opposite direction until we run out of room again."

"Right. We tack back and forth and hope we can stay away from the rocks."

"Then we have a plan," she says, moving out from under the dodger's shelter to the steering station.

Gripping the wheel with both hands, she tells him, "I'm ready."

Michael

The wind returns with a deafening roar, blasting through the cove's entrance. After years on the sea, he understands this wind as power without remorse.

He clips his tether into the jack line. The wind is too strong for him to stand now, so he scrambles on all fours to the main mast and raises the storm sail. On either side of him, waves sweep the side decks with white foam carpets. As he crawls back to the cockpit, the sail flogs violently, adding to the frightening racket the rigging makes.

He cranks the sail in until it stops flogging. "I'm going to the bow now," he shouts to her. He sees color drain from her face. "I'll be careful."

Inching across the side deck as the boat heaves and pitches, he crawls forward. At the bow, he stares at the frothing tumult raking the cove's surface. From here he has a clear view of huge breaking waves rolling through the entrance, their tops blown off into spume and spindrift. The storm has reached another level of destruction, and, for a moment, its violence and strange beauty hold him fascinated.

He can't believe the conditions are so terrible inside the cove, and he finds himself awed by the forces at work. He's confronted by a huge open-mouthed wind that refuses to moderate. The ceaseless rush of the breaking seas is not so much terrifying as chilling, a reminder to him the sea is without mercy.

Turning toward the cockpit, he signals her for more throttle, then cranks the anchor windlass. A larger wave breaks over the bow and frigid water forces its way inside his foul weather jacket and down his back. The bow rises on each wave and then falls away under him, leaving him suspended, then crashing back to the deck on his knees. The image of a bronco rider, one hand waving free on a bucking bull, flashes to him.

He motions to her for more power and, as *Shearwater* staggers forward, he feels the anchor break out from the mud bottom. *Charlotte is solid on the helm*, he thinks. Another wave breaks over the bow. This time freezing water is driven up the arms of his foul weather jacket. Inside his foulies, his clothes are sodden. He feels the wind trying to blow him off the foredeck, into the sea.

As fast as he can ratchet the windlass, he raises the anchor until it's secured in the bow chock. Then he scrambles back to the cockpit, aided this time by the wind pushing him along the side deck. "We can turn the engine off now!" he shouts to her.

He watches as she reaches down and pulls the kill switch. The engine sputters, stops and the alarm rings until she turns the key off.

Freed from the anchor, *Shearwater* rolls over and accelerates towards the rocks, the wind shoving her down the cove.

"She's not responding!" Charlotte shouts to him.

"Hang on!" he shouts back.

He slides next to her, places his hands on hers and spins the wheel over. "Fall off like this until the sails fill," he tells her.

As the boat turns onto the new heading, the wind buoys out the sails, and suddenly the masts lean over and the deck slants beneath them. Only a dozen yards off the rocks, the boat stops its backward motion and begins to claw its way forward, almost imperceptibly at first but then with more speed.

"She's doing it!" Charlotte yells.

But as the boat continues to heel over, she grabs his arm, alarm on her face.

"Eight thousand pounds of lead in the keel," he reassures her. "She won't turn turtle."

"She's not a turtle," Charlotte says, a faint smile of relief on her lips.

For the first time since they both laid across the inflatable on the foredeck, he laughs.

"No," he says, smiling. "She's a shearwater."

Charlotte

"She's sailing!" Charlotte shouts above the wind, feeling the ketch's power through the soles of her feet and through the wheel, which seems to have a will of its own as it twists in her hands.

"*You're* sailing!" he shouts back.

She grins. "It's been thirty years."

Under the wind's force on the sails, the boat begins to gain distance from the rocks, smashing its bow into the on-coming waves. Now it's a fairer fight, she tells herself. It's not just the waves pounding *Shearwater*, the ketch can punch back. She takes comfort from this, even though every time they slam into a wave, the boat shudders and almost stops. But yard by yard *Shearwater* thrusts forward into the devouring walls of water.

Through the wheel, she can feel the strength of the waves as they push on the rudder, at times with such force the wheel threatens to break free from her white-knuckled grasp.

"How long on this course," she asks.

He glances across the cove and then bends close to her ear. "Ten minutes, maybe fifteen. You warm enough?"

"I'm okay. The wheel keeps turning in my hands. Fighting me."

"Winds too strong. Even for the tiny sails we have up."

She watches him climb onto the cockpit coaming on the high side and feels his weight reduce a bit of the boat's heeling.

He cups his hands around his mouth. "I'm right here if you need me."

But she doesn't need him now. Despite the screaming wind and battering waves, and the boat feeling almost out of control, she's exhilarated by its responsiveness, how alive *Shearwater* feels.

After fifteen minutes, Michael eases off the cockpit coaming and comes to her at the wheel. "We need to tack," he says in a loud voice.

She nods and watches as he wraps the opposite sheet around the port winch.

Turning towards her, he says "Ready."

She spins the wheel until the bow comes through the wind and the boat falls off onto the opposite tack, heeling hard. She remembers to bring the wheel back to the center, and the boat stops turning.

The sails flog as they cross from one side to the other, making a deafening racket, while Michael inserts a handle into the top of the winch and cranks fast until the storm sail fills.

The boat lurches forward on the new course, like a live animal on whose back she's riding.

Michael places the winch handle in its holder and stands next to her at the wheel. "That was a clean tack," he says, approvingly.

"If the motion wasn't so violent, I'd be thrilled by this," she says.

"These are hellacious conditions."

Minutes later she points toward the approaching shore. "We need to tack again," she shouts to him. "Ready?"

He smiles, wraps the loose line around the starboard winch and shouts back, "Ready."

They repeat the previous maneuver in reverse, and she's aware of how much the two of them resemble dancers in a tight choreography, both attending to the needs of the boat as they move.

She spins the wheel with more confidence now, and they fall onto the opposite tack.

When he's stored the winch handle and climbed onto the high side of the cockpit, he cups his hands around his mouth and says, "We do this every ten or fifteen minutes."

"How long?" she asks.

"Until this damn storm blows through."

Michael

Instead of easing, the storm gathers strength.

The wind stiffens, rising to the next level of mayhem.

He squints into the stinging rain and sees towering waves break and foam and hiss, as they pound *Shearwater's* hull with growing force. The wind seems to toy with the boat, as if the eight-ton vessel was a child's plaything.

Hour after hour they tack back and forth. Trying to hold the ketch's position in the middle of the cove under a torn angry sky, filled with scudding clouds.

By now, his head aches. Salt burns his throat. The gunnels are awash with white water. He struggles to keep his balance as he moves across the cockpit from one winch to the other, while Charlotte fights the wheel.

They tack and tack and tack…until he's sick of it. Despite sailing gloves, his hands are blistered. His arms and shoulders scream from grinding the winches. He thinks the wound in his back may have re-opened and is tempted to switch places with Charlotte. But he won't do that until he can't raise his arms at all. He knows she must be drained, standing at the wheel hour after hour, the boat rolling and lurching as heaving walls of water smash into the bow and then cascade down the side decks, each time *Shearwater* groaning and staggering in protest, but somehow driving forward.

"You must be exhausted," he says, between two tacks in the early afternoon.

"Beat to pieces," she says. "But I've never felt this alive."

He sees she's without fear. Knows she's a woman with whom he could spend his life. And that he'll always remember this as Charlotte's storm.

His stomach is hollow with hunger, and he imagines she must be hungry too. At the end of a tack, he ducks below and brings up coffee and sandwiches. He hands her a sandwich while she stands at the helm and places the thermos in a holder, under the wheel. Sitting on the cockpit coaming, he wolfs down his sandwich in time to be ready for the next tack.

When she's finished eating and they're between tacks, he brings a bottle of water to the cockpit.

The afternoon wears on with endless tacking, the sky remaining dark, threatening. He wants to believe the wind is lessening, that the waves are beginning to flatten. *We're meant to live.*

He moves to her at the wheel. "Do you think it's going down?"

"I hope so."

"We might be out of danger. I should get the anchor ready, between the next two tacks."

She gives him a thumbs up.

When they've come about and started on the new heading, he clips into the jack line and scrambles toward the bow. But just as he passes the mainmast, a tremendous windblast hits them. He hears a loud pop at the top of the mast.

He looks up and sees the top hank of the storm sail has broken loose from the mast track. He watches in fascinated horror as one by one the lower hanks break away, like a zipper opening. Suddenly the sail is free, streaming from the mast like a loose flag. Immediately, the bow falls off, and *Shearwater* lurches backward, rapidly gaining speed toward the rocks.

"Michael!" Charlotte screams, "I have no helm."

"Hang on!" he yells.

Charlotte

For the first time, uncontrollable fear plucks at her as *Shearwater* races downwind with increasing speed, out of control. With no sails or engine, the wheel does nothing, but she hangs onto it to keep from being swept into the sea. She grips the wheel so tightly her palms sting.

She sees Michael struggle to stay on the boat, grasping for handholds as he slides on the deck, and his legs go under the lifelines. Her mouth goes dry. Only the jack line is holding him to the boat now. The ketch accelerates toward the rocks. She pushes down the panic rising in her throat.

Finally, she sees Michael pull himself back on board and exhales the breath she's been holding.

"We have to start the engine!" he yells to her as he grapples his way aft and into the cockpit.

"We'll destroy it," she shouts, the words barely clearing her mouth before the wind snatches them away.

"Without the engine, we're lost anyway," he tells her, turning the key.

Looking behind her, she sees huge waves smashing ashore in billows of spray. *This storm is trying to kill us*. A certain fatalism comes over her, a strange calm.

The engine coughs once…twice…then turns over.

She slams the throttle forward and spins the wheel.

Seconds later—an eternity later—*Shearwater's* backward momentum slows, then stops, the ketch's transom just yards off the rock-strewn beach.

Slowly the ketch claws forward and for the second time today, she thinks *safe for the moment. But for how long?*

"How much fuel?" she asks.

He kneels and studies the gauge. "Maybe an hour."

"What do we do?"

"Try to motor almost to the entrance and then set the anchor."

"Will it hold?"

"Only if the wind lightens."

She thinks about this. If the anchor lets go with no engine, they'll have only as long as it takes for the wind to drive *Shearwater* down the cove again. This time to the ketch's certain destruction. And theirs too.

Michael

They're most of the way across the cove when the fuel gauge shows empty. He expects the engine to die at any moment. "We have to drop the anchor," he shouts to her.

She looks at him, mute. His heart goes to her. But he must get to the bow before the engine dies.

On his way forward he wants to believe the wind is lessening. Tries to convince himself the gusts are not as frequent, the waves flattening a bit.

The sky to the north has lightened near the horizon. Taking it as a sign, he unlocks the anchor windlass, turns, raises his right hand and watches as Charlotte brings the bow into the wind. Then he lets the anchor go.

The line screams out of the chain locker until the anchor hits bottom. By then *Shearwater* is already backing down. He picks out a tall tree on shore and watches until it stops moving relative to the boat.

He shouts to her, "It's set."

He hears her kill the engine for the final time, the warning bell shrieking until she can turn the key off. He imagines it's quieter, although the wind still screams in the rigging and waves continue to pound Shearwater's bow. At least the storm sail isn't flogging, he tells himself now that he's retrieved the torn sail and stuffed it below. He wants to believe the huge gust that tore the sail from its track was the storm blowing itself out.

He returns to the cockpit where Charlotte has collapsed under the dodger.

"I think the wind's gone down a bit," she says, hopefully.

"The waves too," he says, dropping down next to her.

"As long as the anchor holds."

"I think it will," he reassures her. He's filled with deep relief.

She puts her head against his shoulder. They sit together in utter exhaustion. Most of an hour passes before they realize that, with a suddenness equal to its arrival, the storm is departing in earnest. The wind drops to under thirty knots and the waves calm. Gaps of blue sky appear in the low scudding clouds.

With nothing more to do but trust the anchor, she goes below to change into dry clothes while he remains in the cockpit long enough to convince himself the storm is truly blown out.

He joins her in the main cabin. "It's over," he says in a tired voice. He removes his sailing gloves and peels off his foul weather jacket and his red overalls. Storing his foulies in the wet locker, along with his sea boots, he pulls off his woolen sweater. Then he lights the kerosene lamps and sits next to her on the settee.

"We saved her," she says, a hint of triumph in her voice.

He puts his arms around her, feels her wet hair on his face. "You have no idea how much that means to me."

"I think I do," she says quietly.

He reaches for her hands.

"Your hands are blistered," she says, turning his palms upward.

"Even with sailing gloves," he says. "But I'm more worried about my back. It felt like the wound might have opened."

"Let me look," she says.

He rises from the settee. "I'll turn up the heater. Try to get the cabin warm."

After tending to the heater, he removes his wet shirt.

"It's opened a bit," she tells him. "Do you have bandages?"

He searches for the first aid kit, finds it, and then sits next to her while she applies a dressing. Her hands are warm and smooth.

He turns around to kiss her.

"Not yet, Michael."

He studies her face. Sees no clues to what she's thinking. He pulls on a dry T-shirt.

"There's something you haven't told me," she says, moving across the narrow space between the berths and sitting on the port settee, opposite him.

"What do you mean?" he asks.

"Something you said during the storm, about sailing allowing you to forget. And when we had dinner and walked on the beach that first time. I saw pain about losing your wife. But there was something else. Something hidden, that you've skirted in all our conversations. That you didn't want to tell me. Is it the war?"

"Yes. How do you know?" he asks.

"The shadow behind your eyes."

He swallows hard. Doesn't trust himself to speak.

"I want to know you completely, Michael. No secrets."

He looks at the cabin sole, at the alternating strips of teak and holly. He studies the beautifully varnished woods as if they could rescue him, his insides churning. Exhausted as he is, he has no defenses against her.

"I've never told anyone. Not even my parents when I came back from the war."

"We've run out of time to hide things from each other," she says, quietly.

A great heaviness comes over him. It crushes the breath out of him. Makes him remember August 1, 1943, a moonless night in the Solomon Islands. He knows she's looking at him. He raises his gaze from the cabin sole and stares into her jade-colored eyes, flecks of light from the kerosene lamps glinting there. She's waiting. Patient. Not pressing him. *What do you have to lose*, he asks himself. *You don't know if you'll ever see her again.*

"We were in the Solomons," he begins, in a voice so soft she leans forward across the narrow space between them. "There were reports of an enemy destroyer in the area, and the squadron commander ordered two of our PT boats to try to find it. One of them was John Kennedy's boat. The other was mine."

Waves left by the storm slap against the hull. She waits, sitting across from him, hands folded in her lap, her eyes fixed on him.

"In a foray three days earlier, I suffered an arm wound, a bullet graze. Maybe you noticed that scar."

"I did," she nods.

"I didn't want to tell you about it."

"I know," she says, her voice gentle.

He looks down at the teak and holly sole again. "The wound wasn't serious, but the medical officer ordered me to take off a week. That I shouldn't go on any missions until it was fully healed and no danger of infection. Infection was a big problem out there. I argued with him. Told him I didn't want any restrictions about going on missions. In the end, he left it up to me when I would return to my boat."

He stops, the lump in his throat too thick to force the words out.

She reaches across the narrow aisle and lays a hand on his arm. Something about that simple gesture relaxes the muscles in his throat.

"I was torn. I wanted to be with my men. The wound wasn't that bad. But at the last minute I decided to stay behind... worried I wasn't a hundred percent and might compromise the mission. At least that's the excuse I gave myself."

She moves across the aisle and sits next to him on the starboard settee. He feels relieved she isn't looking directly at him now. *Maybe, she's not seeing my shame. Or my guilt.*

"Our PT boats didn't have radar and were surprisingly primitive. Flimsy really, but extremely fast and maneuverable."

He feels her sitting next to him, feels her warmth, and the words pour out of him now. "That night, there was no moon, no light. A destroyer came out of nowhere. It rammed Jack's boat first, cut it in half, spilling all the men into the water, killing some of them instantly. Then it turned and rammed my boat, spilling my men into the water too, both boats sinking in minutes."

She says nothing. Just listens.

"Bob Sweeney, my co-skipper, died immediately," he chokes on his words. "That was supposed to be me, Charlotte. He died, and I lived."

He fights down the sobs rising in his throat, feels her hand on his arm and tries to take strength from it.

"Most of the men in the water were injured and couldn't swim well, or at all. Jack spent hours rescuing as many as he could, including two of my men." His voice is shaking now. "He dragged them through the water with a belt, pulling them to safety on a small island a few miles away."

In the soft light from the kerosene lamps, his head sinks into his hands. He feels sick with sorrow and regret. "I should have gone on that mission, Charlotte. I'm a strong swimmer. If I had survived the ramming, I could have saved some of my men. The way Jack did." He hears the humiliation in his voice. "It should have been me that night," he whispers, "instead of Bob Sweeney."

Her arms come around him now. The nearness of her breath—tears spring into his eyes. He turns his head away, doesn't want her to see him like this.

"You can't know that," she says, her voice soft. "There's no way to ever know that."

"My wife's death. Her botched surgery? It felt like retribution for my not going on that mission."

"That's just not true, Michael. It was war. Terrible things happened. And your wife's death was a tragedy. An accident."

"I've tried to let it go."

"Can you forgive yourself?"

"I have tried." He wipes the tears away, turns back to Charlotte.

"Until you forgive yourself, Michael, you will always be withholding part of your heart. How can you love me now, living in the past?"

"I want you, Charlotte. More than anything or anyone I've ever wanted. I need you."

"Then let your guilt go," she says. "You did what you could."

He's choked with sadness.

"The war did its brutal work," she tells him. "The way all wars do."

She pulls him close.

"There's no meaning to be found in any of it," she says. "Let it go, Michael."

Charlotte

A full yellow moon has risen in the eastern sky, visible through the starboard portlights, and she realizes this enormous moon foreshadows the month's highest tide two days from now. She thinks about how little time they have together before he departs and wraps her arms around his shoulders to hold him.

She feels him sobbing, his body shaking in her arms. She kisses the side of his face, strokes his hair.

"There was a reason they made you captain of that PT boat. You were a leader," she tells him. "But you were wounded."

When his shaking subsides, he turns to her. She kisses him softly. She thinks she must look half drowned but that isn't what she sees in his eyes. There's no mistaking his gaze and she melts under its intensity.

She hardly knows this man, yet she's risked her life for him. The exhilaration she feels at having survived the storm counters her fatigue. *We're alive. Together, we saved Shearwater.*

She surprises herself and pulls him to her, raises her face and kisses him again. His mouth tastes salty, like the sea, but sweet at the same time.

His hands slide down to her waist, to her hips—she begins to unravel.

He pulls the bottom of her shirt over her head. She lifts her arms to help him and then unfastens her bra. Now she's opening—like a spinnaker opening, filling with a warm wind.

When her breasts come free, he exhales a sharp breath.

Whatever defenses she's erected crumble. She wants more of him, more proof she's still alive. She wants his skin on hers, his warmth against her.

In the cabin's steaming heat, they're both driven by a frantic haste, stripping off each other's clothes, until they stand naked in the moonlight, circles floating through the portlights.

He kneels and encircles her waist with his arms and draws her breasts to his lips. A tremor shivers through her. She no longer has the strength in her legs to stand. She lets her weight melt into his embrace, her fingers resting along his back, careful to avoid the wound.

For a moment she wonders how long it's been since he's made love to a woman.

She moves her hands down his back, over his smooth skin. In the pale moonlight, she remembers pulling him into her living room—the dead weight of him—her exertion, the wild pounding of her heart.

He reaches down and tugs on the bottom of the starboard berth. It comes forward in his hands, covering most of the center aisle. Of its own accord, the back cushion of the starboard berth falls back to form a double berth.

He lowers her onto it and kneels beside her. As he bends to her belly, his lips grazing her skin, she reaches over with her right arm and caresses his bare shoulders. She needs to touch him, to be closer. With her fingers, she explores his back, the bones in his spine. Through half-shuttered lids, she sees moonlight streaming through the portlights. She's floating. Adrift.

She savors his patient, languorous movements, his caresses. His mouth finds each of the indentations in her neck, the flat place between her breasts, the heat of her parted thighs. She shudders under the soft press of his lips there. There's urgency in her desire for him now.

Finally, he moves over her, supporting his weight. Raising one hand to the side of his face, she traces the line of his chin, his lips, the tiny scar under his eye. In the moonlight, her insides float—like a leaf on a slow current.

Again, she runs her fingers through his hair, behind his neck, over his rugged shoulders.She closes her eyes, feels his hands on her, almost burning her skin. Feels him move over her. She's not thinking about what any of this means. She's past that now.

"We're alive," she says in a hoarse whisper.

An instant before she closes her eyes and feels him enter her, he whispers, "And you're more beautiful than ever."

Slowly he moves his hips, and she feels a wind gathering, flowing through her. Carrying her aloft. She pushes off the berth to meet him, a great pressure inside, every nerve alive.

She pulls him down to her and smells his scent: sea moss and white sand beaches. Under her fingers, his skin is polished driftwood. His breath ragged on her shoulder, his arms tense around her. She arches her head once. And again. Nothing matters except this moment. She's buoyant, open. The language of his body stirs inside her, lapping at the edges of desire.

He moves on her like the rhythm of the sea: rising and falling. The wind inside her howls now, screams as its pressure builds somewhere at her center—pushing forward a wave of desire which hovers, cresting, cresting, and then breaks free, radiating out from her core, a flooding tide coursing through her limbs, released onto a vast endless sea.

Michael

Afterwards, feeling her lips on his shoulder, tender on his skin, he remembers the way her fingers dug into his flesh, the strength of her thighs pulling him to her. For a long time, he stays fixed, not moving—not wanting to move—until her arms slip from his back, and she releases him.

In the moonlight, the skin on her chest is mottled, her face flushed. He feels her tremble and turns on his side, pressing against her in the berth. He knows that finally his long voyage has reached its end. He's found what he hadn't known he'd been searching for. Found it in her arms. An acceptance. A profound peace.

They lie together, dozing for a while, as if gathering strength. Then he reaches for her again. Even more slowly, savoring every sensation of her skin, her earthy scent, her sounds. Her whispered "I love you," and his repeating the words back.

They sleep. He isn't sure how long. Until he awakens to her saying, "I'm cold."

He slides away, covering her with a sheet, then pulls a wool blanket from a locker and spreads it over her. She shivers in her half-sleep and draws it over her breasts.

"I need to check topsides," he says. "Make sure we're safe until morning. I won't be long."

"Hurry."

He turns the furnace setting higher and pulls on a pair of jeans and his foul-weather jacket. Then he goes out into the cockpit and forward to the bow. The clouds have moved off to the south, and the full moon is almost directly overhead, more white than yellow. The outline of the ketch is clear in the moonlight. At the bow, he checks to make sure the small anchor is holding, and the additional chafing protection is working. Satisfied *Shearwater* is not going anywhere, he returns to the cockpit.

As he opens the hatch, a smile spreads across his face. Not only have they survived the storm, but when he wakes in the morning, he won't be alone.

When he comes down the companionway, moonlight streams through the hatch. He sees she's fallen asleep, her hair spilled around her head on the pillow. Under the covers, she lies curled into herself, facing outward, both hands hidden under her right cheek. *An angel*, he thinks.

He removes his sailing jacket, studies her relaxed face, her slightly parted mouth. He's flooded with desire for her again. But it's more than physical this time. He wants to reach behind the essential mystery of her and see into her soul.

Carefully, so as not to wake her, he kneels and puts his lips to her forehead. He rests his face there for a moment. In the cabin's stillness, he finds it hard to believe that only hours earlier they had battled the storm together. A day in which he'd faced his possible end. Then found his life. And Charlotte's love.

Instinctively, his hand gathers a thick strand of her long hair. He lets it sift slowly through his fingers. This is a woman he loves deeply. He's struck by the absolute certainty of that.

She stirs in her sleep, and he lifts his face from hers. Stepping softly, he flicks on the navigator's station light, filling the cabin with its soft red glow—he doesn't want her to lose her footing in the dark cabin if she wakes during the night.

He puts in two of the hatch boards and rigs the mosquito netting, then strips off his deck shoes and jeans. He slips in beside her and tucks the edges of the blanket under the settee cushion. Gently, he pulls back her hair to see her face, already softened with sleep, wildly beautiful in the navigator light's red glow. He feels love growing, deepening. And there's so much for them to talk about.

Tomorrow.

Charlotte

Waking in the berth, it takes her a few seconds to remember she's in *Shearwater*'s main cabin, surrounded by warm teak and the comfortable furnishings of the ketch. Yellow sunlight streams in through the starboard portlights and the boat lies almost motionless under her, the clean smell of the sea inside the cabin. She glances at her watch. It is already late morning. *Incredible*, she thinks, *I've slept more than eleven hours*. It's the boat's rocking she tells herself, like a hammock swaying in the wind.

She remembers last night—Michael's shoulders above her, framed in moonlight. Was it a dream? No, it was real, and she feels heat in her face.

She swings her legs over the edge of the berth. Was what happened between them merely a reaction to the immense strain the storm had placed on them? Their relief at surviving. She holds her head in her hands, gathering her thoughts.

Finally, she stands, wraps herself in the gray blanket and walks to the companionway. The top hatch board is missing and through the thin gauze of mosquito netting she can see into the cockpit where Michael stands under the boom, naked.

She inhales a sharp breath.

His hands are raised, massaging shampoo into his hair, his chest open to her gaze, the muscles stretched and defined.

In that pose, his nakedness has an innocence about it. When he turns away, she sees the sun reflected on his flank, the slope of his spine. She feels the pulse in her neck beating and remembers how it felt, cradling him between her thighs.

Now, in the cockpit, he turns back towards her, eyes still closed, his fingers working in the shampoo, the dark hair at his groin wet and clinging, his torso gleaming in the sun like a statue.

As she watches, Michael reaches around with his right hand, eyes still closed, for the thin hose dangling from the black sun shower bag, hanging from the boom. When his hand finds it, he opens the valve and water streams over his head, down his arms and chest, between his legs—rinsing the white shampoo suds down his body, onto the teak grate in the cockpit floor.

A dozen memories of her night with him ascend on her, and she etches the image of him showering in the cockpit in her mind forever.

Since David died, she's not felt this kind of passion. Michael is like oxygen when she's with him, allowing her to breathe again, like the lightness she feels on Keller Peak, not just free but wild.

Then her thoughts turn gray. Michael will leave the island tomorrow on the highest tide. That will be the end.

Unless I go with him.

She raises her eyes to Eagle Cove's entrance, opening her imagination to the unseen expanse of the sea beyond, and the voyage she and Michael could share.

Despite her deep love for Tommy, and her affection for Ben—despite the responsibilities and attachments binding her to Cambria Island—in her heart, she knows a part of her, growing huge inside her now, craves that freedom.

Aches for it.

Michael

In the cabin he finds her dressed, combing out her hair.

"You're up," he says, smiling.

She throws him a mock frown, "You might have woken me."

"You needed sleep. We both did. I'll make breakfast now. A real meal. You must be starved."

"I'm really hungry," she acknowledges. "How can I help?"

"Keep me company," he says, pulling what he needs from the coolers and bringing out a cutting board from behind the galley sink. "Talk to me."

"What about?"

"You know what about," he says, gazing directly at her from the galley where he slices mushrooms and bits of ham on the cedar board.

"Tomorrow?"

"Yes."

"Must we talk about that?"

"I think we need to," he responds, whipping pancake batter in a bowl. "I have only one chance to take *Shearwater* out of here for at least another month. And Ben and Tommy are returning. What if I'm still here?"

"I don't know," she says. "I can't make any sense of this."

He sets aside the pancake batter and moves across the cabin to sit next to her. "Come with me, Charlotte." He takes one of her hands in his. "We'll sail the world. I'll show you the most amazing places. Tasmania, the Galapagos, Bora Bora, Sumatra, the atolls in Fiji, the great barrier reef in Australia, the stunning southern island of New Zealand. In Tahiti, you can see those Gauguin paintings you admire so much. And you can paint to your heart's desire."

He sees her studying his face.

"I can show you dozens, no, hundreds of secluded anchorages in the south Pacific," he continues, taking both her hands in his now. "No other boats there yet. Come with me and Orion and we'll have an incredible life together on *Shearwater*. We'll live in the moment."

She meets his gaze directly, and the jade in her eyes startles him all over again. "How do you know we'll be good together?" she asks, earnestly. "We've known each other for only eight days. Eight days, Michael!"

"Do you love me?" he asks abruptly.

He sees her hesitate.

Then, "I don't understand it. But I do love you."

"It makes me happy to hear you say those words. Come with me. I will be good for you. And for certain you'll be good for me. We proved so much in the last thirty-six hours. We proved everything."

"You're convinced of that?" she asks.

"Let me tell you about the dream I had last night," he responds. "It was so vivid it seemed real. Earlier I had dreamed of you as a butterfly. Did I tell you that?"

"I don't think so."

"In last night's dream, your butterfly wings kept growing and expanding. They grew and spread into the wide, soaring wings of a shearwater!"

Her eyes shine now.

He slides closer to her. "Then you spread those shearwater wings and lofted into the sky and flew out over the sea, free and soaring." He softens his voice. "In my dream, after a while, you saw *Shearwater*, far out on the ocean. You circled, and then you landed on the ketch and changed back into Charlotte. You were with me."

He sees her eyes glistening and takes her into his arms. "Come with me, Charlotte," he whispers. "We'll be shearwaters together."

Charlotte

She watches as he rises from the settee and moves to the galley. He lights a burner under a large skillet and then finishes whipping the pancake batter. She sees him slide the sliced mushrooms and ham bits off the cutting board into the pancake mix, stirring it again.

"Are you sure I can't help," she asks from her place on the starboard settee.

"Let me do this for you, it gives me pleasure," he says, placing a hand under the sink faucet, wetting his fingers. He flicks his fingers at the skillet and water droplets sizzle and skitter across the pan.

He pours the batter into three good-sized pancakes, and when those are done on both sides to a golden brown, he pours three more.

"Why don't we eat in the cockpit," he says, handing her a short stack and a coffee cup, steam rising from it.

Ham and mushrooms folded into pancakes is a combination she's never had before. Sitting in the cockpit with her plate, she decides the pancakes taste amazing, and the coffee is among the best she's had. Probably her ravishing hunger, she thinks.

They take their time eating under a transparent blue sky, savoring their first real meal since before the storm, while rough-winged swallows dart and swoop over the water around them.

After stowing his breakfast plate below, Michael leans against the bulkhead at the front of the cockpit and dozes in the warm sun while she wrestles with her thoughts, the impossible decision facing her.

She thinks about Michael's offer to take her away to a life of adventure and exploration. Sitting here next to him on *Shearwater*, she's drawn to his impassioned proposal with a force that's overwhelming. Does she really need to fight this, or should she go ashore and pack her things and bring them aboard *Shearwater*? Write long letters to Tommy and Ben, trying to explain.

She wants to kiss him, but instead reaches across and lays a hand on his arm. His eyes fly open.

"What is it?" he asks, sitting up. "Something wrong?"

"I can't leave Tommy," she says in a whisper.

He opens his mouth to respond but says nothing. Instead, he moves to her side of the cockpit and sits next to her.

She thinks of a decade of diary entries she's made about her son. "Tommy's been my life for these eleven years," she says, softly. "He's still my life."

The smell of the ocean is sharp in the air around them. A family of sea otters swim past. The sun is warmer now and time seems to slow.

"He's old enough now to understand this," Michael says quietly, in the deep, resonant voice she loves. "And he *will* pull away from you, anyway."

The glistening head of a seal bobs in the distance.

She's slow to answer. Then she tells him, "I believe part of that. In the last year or two Tommy *has* moved more toward Ben. But I haven't seen any signs of rebellion. Not yet anyway."

"It'll happen," Michael says. "And it will be just as hard for you then as it would be now."

She considers the truth in this. The progression she's seen with the sons of other women on the island. But right now, she feels Tommy is still hers. "It's natural for a son to become more independent from his mother," she says, "of course I understand that. But it's not natural for a mother to leave her eleven-year-old son."

Michael hesitates. Then he says, "I know this is an impossible choice. I've seen how much you love Tommy. Whatever you decide, I'll always love you, Charlotte."

"And I'll always love you, Michael."

"But if I leave," she says, retreating for the moment from talking about Tommy, "Ben would be crushed. He wouldn't understand at all. He'd see it as the worst kind of betrayal, and he'd never forgive me."

Michael looks out across the water, then back to her. In a voice so quiet she can barely hear him above the cries of gulls soaring over the cove, he asks, "Then you've made your decision to stay?"

She takes his hand in hers, feels the blisters from winch grinding, the warmth of him coming through his fingers. "I'm torn to pieces."

A great blue heron lifts from the beach, squawking, and flies over them, legs trailing.

"My life here has become closed in. My sense of excitement about the world has just slipped away." She turns to him. "You've aroused all that again."

He squeezes her hand. "Come me with Charlotte," he says in a voice bordering on pleading. "I want you in my life, more than I've ever wanted anything."

"If we could raise the anchor right now…today…and sail out that entrance and not look back, I think I could do it." She turns toward the cove's entrance. "I think I could go with you."

"Tomorrow afternoon is the tide *Shearwater* needs."

"I know," she says.

"You still have time," he says. "And we have these hours together. Let's make the most of them."

Michael

"I need to dive the boat," he says quietly, rising from the cockpit seat, "checking for damage from coming over the entrance reef."

"Now?" she asks, looking up.

"With overhead sun, visibility in the water is best now," he says. "As soon as I'm done, we can go ashore and check on Orion and Toby."

She glances across the water toward the house. "I have to see how our property fared in the storm."

He opens a cockpit locker and removes a wet suit. "It won't take long, but it would help if you would stand by while I'm down there."

She gestures toward the water. "Of course, I'll help you."

"I'll be quick," he promises.

While she waits in the cockpit, he goes below, undresses, and pulls on his wet suit, positioning goggles on his forehead. Back in the cockpit he pushes his feet into large swim fins.

"All set?" she asks.

"I just need my weight belt."

He straps on his weight belt and moves to the stern pulpit and opens the gate in it. "I'll go in here," he tells her. "And come up to the rope ladder on the starboard side. Just keep an eye out for me. I can stay down for about ninety seconds."

After pulling in half a dozen deep breaths, he jumps feet first off the transom, letting the weight belt pull him down through the translucent green water. With the mid-day sun above him, he can see the hull clearly and is relieved to find only a few barnacles. Head down, he kicks hard, and reaches the bottom of the keel. Now he can run his hand along the keel timber, from the stern toward the bow. Carefully, he looks and feels for cracks or breaks in the hard wood as he swims forward. But finding none, he kicks upward, pulling in a big breath when he surfaces.

Charlotte is bent over the rail, and he sees a look of relief cross her face as he swims to the rope ladder and grabs hold.

"Well?" she asks.

"Looks good," he calls up to her. "But I'm going to check one more time to be certain."

"Be careful."

He gives her a thumbs up, and after pulling in deeper breaths, bends at the waist and scissor kicks down toward the bottom of the keel. This time he starts forward and works his way aft, running his hand along the smooth wood and pulling himself down so he can visually inspect as well. Again, he finds nothing that concerns him. He kicks hard for the surface, climbs the rope ladder, and scrambles onto the deck.

He pulls off his goggles and fins and releases his weight belt. "I don't feel or see any damage. Just one indentation, and it's not structural."

"I'm sure you're relieved," she says.

He nods. "*Shearwater*'s ready. I'll rinse off and change and we can go ashore."

When he's changed into shorts and a long-sleeved shirt, he lifts the starboard settee cushion and opens a small locker hidden underneath it. He removes a metal box from inside the locker and sets it down on the chart table. When he opens the box, he sees the eight-inch scrimshaw narwal he carved years ago, from a large whale's tooth he found lying on a beach in Tasmania.

He brings the narwhal with him as he climbs out into the cockpit where Charlotte's been waiting. He sits down next to her and holds out the carving.

"I want you to have this," he says, laying the narwhal in her upturned palm.

"It's beautiful," she says, slowly turning the ivory over in her hands. "You made this?"

He nods. "I spent several months in Mexico one year waiting for hurricane season to end. Lots of time for carving."

"It's stunning," she says, tracing her fingers over the slender whale and its long horn.

"Unicorns of the sea," he tells her. "Some think narwals bring good luck."

"Are you sure I should take this, Michael?" She raises her head to look at him. "All the work to carve it. It's a museum piece."

"I want you to have it. You've given me so much."

"What have I given you?" she asks.

"Freedom," he answers. "To finally live my life with an open heart."

Her eyes shine.

"I can let go of my guilt," he says. "It'll take time. But I'm determined now to put what happened in the war behind me."

She leans over and kisses him.

He watches as she carefully sets the narwal down on the cockpit seat. Then she reaches around behind her neck with both hands and removes a slender silver chain that holds a gold locket. She slips the locket off the chain and hands it to him.

"Then I want you to keep this," she says.

He takes it from her, presses the tiny knob on the side and the locket springs open. Inside is a photo of her from her shoulders up. He thinks it must have been taken quite a few years ago. Her hair isn't as long, and her face is younger. She's looking straight at the camera, a hint of defiance in her eyes.

"I'll treasure this," he says. "I'd hope the narwal, and this locket, are what we share together for the rest of our lives."

"I know," she says, her face serious now. "Part of me wants that too."

Charlotte

On the foredeck, she helps him untie the inflatable and together they lower it into the water and lead it back to the transom. She watches as he lifts the small outboard from the stern pulpit, climbs down and clamps it to the dinghy's stern.

"Do you have everything?" he asks.

She nods and passes him her duffel bag. "I packed the scrimshaw in there," she tells him. "It'll be safer than me holding it."

He starts the outboard and they motor toward the dock, scattering wood ducks and gulls as they cross the cove. They unload at the dock, and she lets him carry the duffel. The tide is high now, the dock ramp almost horizontal, and they hurry up the path.

As they approach the house, Orion barks loudly from the dog run behind the shop. Michael rushes ahead and lets his Husky out.

"He's probably starved," she says coming up to them and patting Orion's flanks. "Dogs never ration food the way cats do. I'll bring him more food after I find Toby, and check for any damage to the house."

"We can wait on the porch," he tells her.

She finds Toby curled on the living room couch, half the food she left in the kitchen for him still uneaten.

She opens the storm shutters, checks around for damage, and then goes upstairs and turns off the lights in Tommy's room. The storm's terror in the dark night rushes back to her. She pushes it away.

Downstairs, she makes a bowl for Orion and takes it out on the porch.

"How's Toby?" Michael asks.

"Fine."

"And the house?"

"Can't find any damage. The trees provide a lot of shelter."

"What do you want to do now?" he asks her.

"Climb Keller Peak with you?"

He stares at her and then smiles.

"Afterwards," she says, "I'll make us dinner."

"Candles and music?"

"Of course."

"In that case, we could make dinner together."

"I won't turn that down," she says shouldering her pack.

He points to the pack. "I can carry that," he says.

"No need, it's light.

"What's in it?"

"Only one thing," she says in a teasing voice.

"What?"

"A blanket."

He moves to her and takes her into his arms. "Do we get to finish up there what we started down here?"

"That's the general idea," she says, smiling.

When he pulls her to him, she can feel his arousal.

She says, "We'll never make it up the mountain at this rate."

"In that case, race you to the trailhead."

"You're on," she shouts, already at a full run.

* * *

It takes just over an hour for them to climb the peak. She pushes hard up the trail, under the forest's vaulted canopy, and he keeps pace with her. No matter how fast they climb, Orion always ranges ahead, often straying from the trail and then returning. The high trees are filled with dappled sunlight and hidden songbirds calling in melodic voices.

At the summit, the departing storm has left the atmosphere clean. Transparent. She can see all the way south to the distant white peak of Mount Rainier and north to the mountains behind Vancouver. To the east, Mount Baker looms against the horizon.

"Breath-taking!" Michael says, standing next to her.

She lets her pack drop and removes a thick blanket. Together they spread it on a flat piece of ground and then double fold it.

Pine needles and bits of grass are stuck to Orion's coat from running through the meadow and the forest understory. She watches as Michael brushes the dog off before leading him to the shade behind a large boulder. "Stay, Orion," he tells the Husky.

She makes a pillow on the blanket with her pack and waits for him. As they'd climbed the last switchback, she'd flashed on a scene that happened frequently in art school. Several young women would come into the drawing classes, casually remove their clothes, and then pose nude for the students, the vast majority of whom were men. She can still recall how jealous she was of these women. Not of their bodies, which were little different from hers, after all she was their same age. It was their self-confidence she envied. Their poise. The emotional freedom that allowed them to pose nude in front of a room full of men.

Until now, that kind of confidence had eluded her in intimate relations. She was too young with David, despite how much she loved him. And she certainly never felt like stripping off her clothes for Ben. But today, here on Keller Peak, in the bright sunlight, it's something she wants to do for Michael, the man who has made her feel anything is possible. Who makes her want to stretch her wings and fly, the fantasy she's often had standing here on this mountain.

Now, she watches Michael come to the edge of the blanket and escape from his clothes in a hurry. But then he stops, and she knows it's the look in her eyes that holds him in place. She steps out of her shorts and instead of dropping them on the blanket, she twirls them on one finger and flings them at him.

Surprised, he catches her shorts, and laughs.

Next, slowly, she pulls her shirt off over her head, freeing her breasts, twirling the shirt on a finger before throwing that too.

Standing naked, he catches her shirt with a broad grin on his lips.

She hooks her thumbs in her panties and slowly steps out of them, tossing the filmy fabric to him. Nude now in the open air, inhaling the scent of pine, she's at ease, her long hair clinging to her body. At last, she's free to express herself, her past behind her, even David behind her. It's Michael who's here, watching her ride her own deep current of sensuality.

Now he bends down and places her clothes on the blanket, steps to her and takes her in his arms. His skin is warm, and where his body grazes hers, she feels a jolt of electricity. He kisses her, a lingering kiss, and then lowers her gently to the blanket.

She lies stretched beneath him as he bends his mouth to the indentation between her breasts, then slides his lips down her stomach barely touching her skin, his fingers playing with her earlobes, then feather-light on the insides of her arms, soft, softer. She feels him bring his arms down around her thighs, his hands cupping the swell of her buttocks and drawing her essence to his mouth. Blasted with desire, she buries both hands in his hair and guides him, her body quivering, arching, writhing, as if in a fever, sensation building in her, building, until explosively, she soars out into the clouds, her cries echoing off the granite face of the mountain.

***

Lying on the blanket, her limbs are heavy, languorous, her eyes only half open in the afternoon brightness. She feels as if she's in a dream. One from which she doesn't want to wake.

Michael is on his side next to her, studying her face. She sees love in his eyes, reads it at the edges of his mouth. She traces his lips with one finger, runs her hand through his hair. She props herself up on an elbow and leans over and kisses him.

The freedom of this moment on the mountain makes her push him gently onto his back. She rolls onto him, surprised he's ready for her again. This time she stays on top, straddling him. She feels his hard thighs under her legs and leans her hands down on his shoulders.

She goes slow again, like removing her clothes, unhurried motions of her hips, rotating on him, the subtle feeling of him allowing sensation to build in her core, but holding back, watching his face, the growing tension there, feeling his hands cup her breasts, the pressure inside her growing, like a forceful wind. Still, she holds back, moving faster on him now, eyes closed, feeling the sensation in her expanding, filling her, until she again releases it all in a drumming rush.

* * *

Afterwards, they lie spent on the blanket, only their fingers touching in the hot sun.Nuthatches and juncos and white-crowned sparrows call from the firs and cedars below them. Above them soft, white clouds drift across an azure sky.

For almost an hour they doze in the sun's warmth. She relishes the feel of him along her length and wishes they could lie together like this forever. But a cool breeze comes up the mountain now, and she tells him she's chilled.

They dress, and Michael calls to Orion. The Husky comes to them from behind the shaded boulder, his tail wagging.

On the way down the mountain, neither of them finds words to fill the forest's silence. Perhaps, she thinks, he's already concerned about leaving tomorrow. Or perhaps he doesn't have any energy left for conversation. After the last two days, she wouldn't blame him for that.

As they come down the trail, her senses are heightened. All of her feels alive in a way she has never felt before. But her mood turns somber as they break out of the trees and approach the house. She tries to put it out of her mind, but she can't escape the realization that in less than twenty-four hours she must choose. Between her life with Ben and Tommy.

Or a life with Michael.

Michael

He keeps her company harvesting kale and chard and leeks from her garden. Being with her for this simple act feels completely natural. So much between them already requires no words. As they come up the porch steps and remove their boots, two raucous crows call to each other from opposite sides of the house.

"Noisy corvids," she says.

"They are," he agrees.

In the kitchen, he slices carrots while she chops the chard. Then he sets the table while she sautés celery, onions, and carrots in a big pot. He watches her add garlic, white beans, and broth, and then cover the pot and turn down the flame. It's easy for him to envision her in *Shearwater's* galley, the two of them cooking together in an easy collaboration.

"Ready in about an hour," she says. "We can relax."

She hands him a bottle of pinot and the corkscrew. "That's been gathering dust in a low cupboard, but I'm hoping it's still good," she tells him.

He pulls the cork and pours a little into a glass and sips it. "Maybe a tiny bit off," he says, "but still drinkable."

"Good," she says. "I could use a glass. Or two."

"I know," he says, understanding how time presses her.

While the soup simmers, she puts on the Sinatra record they both like and lights the candles they used last time. He can tell she's trying to recreate the buoyant mood of that evening.

When the soup's done, dinner is slow, relaxed, quiet. Outside a robin is upset at something and lets them know with its drawn-out screeching. The soup warms them from the inside and sates their hunger.

Their dancing afterwards is even slower than dinner, not really moving, just holding each other. He savors the feel of her in his arms, her head resting on his chest. *This is where she belongs.*

When he sees her yawning, and she makes indications of heading upstairs, he asks, "Didn't you tell me that couch pulls out? After our breakfast that first morning."

"I did tell you that. We use it when Ben's family or friends visit."

"Why don't we stay down here then?" For all that he's done with Ben's wife, he can't bring himself to sleep in the man's bed, let alone make love to her there.

She studies his face. "We can do that."

Together they pull out the bed, put on sheets and a blanket.

When they're settled in, she snuggles against him, and he waits for her to start a conversation, but she's too deep in thought or too tired. And he doesn't know what words he could say that wouldn't trivialize what's in his heart.

He knows he can't pressure her to come with him, any more than the fervent proposal he made to her on *Shearwater*. What purpose would it serve?

Charlotte

She lays on the pull-out bed wide-eyed, unable to sleep, counting down the minutes until he must leave, a knot of dread growing inside her as those minutes turn to an hour, then another.

Michael's arms have long since relaxed around her, his breathing deep and even. She slips quietly from the bed and goes down the hall to the desk in her catch-all room. In the dark, she sits in the chair and holds her head in her hands.

At three in the morning she still can't sleep, thinking about Ben and her life with him. Trying to understand the reasons she's allowed herself to spend these eight days with Michael. And how she can feel so much love and passion for him, after such a short time. She knows she needs to come to terms with what's happened in her marriage if she's to make the right decision.

Sitting in the darkness, she remembers when she first came to the island and Ben had been good as his word about allowing her time to try to make art again, and to grieve for her loss of David. At first the novelty of life on Cambria, how different it was from anything she'd experienced before, raised her spirits. But eventually her sadness returned and with it a profound depression. Only the hikes up Keller Peak held any balm for her and even then, on more than one climb, she contemplated what it would be like to end her life by throwing herself off its heights.

On several occasions during those early months, Ben left at the front door of her cabin raisin muffins or chocolate chip cookies he'd baked. And twice he offered to make her dinner. He gave up asking again only after she refused him both times.

That first winter on Cambria, filled with rainy, overcast days, was the low point. The cabin alternated between a cold dampness and suffocating heat when the wood stove was roaring. Adding to her depression was her lack of interest in making art. After her grief led her to cover one large canvas in bursts of black, purples and flaming reds, she couldn't find the energy to paint.

When Spring came with the white-barked alders leafing out and tulips blooming around the cabin, her depression lifted long enough for her to challenge herself about what she really wanted. The answer came from her body, an urge growing inside her for several years was now more insistent as she approached her thirties. She wanted a child. That had been her dream with David, and she realized she could have that with Ben. Despite his shyness, he'd given her enough signs he was interested.

But did she want him? She felt no passion for him, nothing resembling the white-hot fire she'd felt for David, a fire that continued to burn even when he was away at war. But maybe she didn't want that kind of passion again. She'd learned that the pain of losing someone you loved that much was shattering.

And how many times in her life did a woman find that kind of love anyway? Only once was the answer that came back to her.

By then she felt confident Ben would be a dependable husband. He would take care of her and whatever children they had together, and it wasn't hard to send signals to him. Just paying attention to her clothes and hair and how she behaved around him drew his attention. He told her how much he liked her auburn hair and her smile. And she didn't need lessons on how a woman could affect a man as shy as Ben. Sitting in the dark at three-thirty in the morning, she remembers how his whole body shuddered the first time he touched her breast. From there things progressed, but she'd not forgotten something her friend Carla had told her years earlier. Never show a man more sexuality than you think he can handle, Carla had said. Charlotte kept that in mind, allowing Ben to take the lead as their intimacies grew.

At a certain point she made it clear to him things would go no further unless he married her, and he immediately admitted that's what he wanted too and seemed embarrassed he hadn't proposed first. He arranged for a small wedding ceremony in a chapel in Bellingham and afterwards Ben's parents and his friends congratulated them with hugging and good wishes but no rice or garter throwing. It was the furthest thing from an elaborate wedding, but it felt right to her.

That night they stayed in one of the better hotels in Bellingham, and she realized sex might not be central to their marriage. In the early morning, when he came to her side of the bed, she understood that if she wanted to reach her own pleasure, she would have to teach him what worked for her. Although he was eager to please her, their chemistry never quite matched.

But Tommy might have been conceived that morning since he was born nine months later in the Anacortes hospital. Since her mother had died in childbirth, she was fearful before Tommy arrived, but his birth went fine. Six days later they motored back to Cambria Island on Ben's trawler with Tommy's swaddled body tucked in a space behind the starboard settee, sleeping soundly until they reached their dock in Eagle Cove.

Tommy's birth was the pivotal point in her marriage to Ben, when her roles as a wife and mother became clear. Any lingering thoughts she had about pursuing art were put away with the same finality that her art supplies were stored behind a large plastic tarp in one corner of Ben's shop, gathering a growing collection of cobwebs and dust. Only the one painting she'd done when she first arrived on the island hung in their house. She had offered to put that one away too, since for her it was painted out of her bitterness at losing David. But Ben didn't mind hanging it in their living room. To this day she thinks he still doesn't understand the emotions that went into the painting, the symbolism.

In truth, most of her was ready for the shift in her roles, especially for being Tommy's mother. He was a joy to raise, his disposition easy from the start, and she welcomed the chance to see the world through his curious and alert eyes as he grew.

Nor did she mind taking over the labor involved in keeping the big house, making meals, and taking full responsibility for the property while Ben was away fishing for weeks at a time. She was young and strong, and these were the roles played by other fisherman's wives on the island. And of course, she came to love gardening, year by year enlarging the vegetable and ornamental gardens she started when Tommy turned three.

It was only as the years went on and Tommy began to draw away from her that a feeling arose in her that she'd given up too much of herself. Dissatisfaction began to eat at her about how routine her life had become. And when she thought about the canvases and brushes stored in the shop, behind the plastic tarp, she became restless and irritated.

One irritant was Ben's lack of interest in walking with her. The long walks they'd shared every day during that week in Anacortes, when they first met, had played such a large role in knowing him, and in her deciding to go with him. But once they were married, he lost interest in walking, and they never seemed to have the kind of open-ended, extended conversations they'd had in Anacortes. As the years went on, he became distant and more inaccessible.

Increasingly, she found herself thinking about the love she'd had with David. Of course, she knew these were foolish thoughts. It was impossible to have that in her marriage to Ben. Any trace of it was buried now under the routine of their daily lives. But her feelings of discontent grew, especially after she came down from her hikes on Keller Peak. She saw colors and textures and vistas on the summit she wanted to paint. Instead, she needed to go down the mountain and make lunch or dinner for Tommy and Ben or do their laundry.

She fought this simmering resentment growing inside her, but it was on one such hike to the summit, ten years after marrying Ben, that it struck her just how great the cost had been of giving up the creative passion of her youth. This was when she first questioned whether that bargain had been worth it. When she finally admitted to herself how much was her responsibility, for not realizing she had the power to change things, if only she would exercise that power. This was the state of her marriage, and her hidden turmoil, when Michael Cordero sailed *Shearwater* into Eagle Cove and collapsed on her front porch.

No wonder she could fall in love with him in such a short time, she thinks, as she turns on the small lamp in the catch-all room and takes sheets of paper from the middle drawer in the desk.

Michael

When he wakes in the morning, he finds Charlotte is not in the pullout bed with him.

He gets up, puts on his jeans, and walks through the house in bare feet. She's not in the kitchen or the downstairs bathroom. He finds her asleep with her head down on a small desk in a room down the hall. He has no idea how long she's been there, but, under her folded arms, he sees two letters, one addressed to Ben and one to Tommy.

She's coming with me.

Elation floods through him. His breath leaves him.

Gently, he caresses her hair. She stirs then, and when she lifts her head, he sees circles under her eyes.

"How long have you been here?" he asks her.

"All night."

"Oh, Charlotte."

"This is so hard," she says, rising from the chair and letting him hold her. She strokes his face with the tips of her fingers. "I've struggled for hours, trying to find the words to say to them."

He takes her hand and presses it to his lips. "Bring the letters. Let's sit at the dining table, and you can tell me about it. I'll make you breakfast."

"I can't eat anything now," she says.

"Then we'll just talk."

At the dining table she lays the letters face down and sits across from him.

"It's strange, but Tommy's letter was easier," she says in a tired voice. "That surprised me. I thought it would be the harder one. I promised to write to him from every port you and I visit. I told him how much I love him. That I know he will grow into a wonderful young man. That his dad will take care of him. I promised him that when we come back this way, he can join us on *Shearwater* for as long as he wants." She throws him a quick penetrating look across the table. The morning sunlight streaming through the kitchen window catches her eyes, making them very green. "Is that something you can honor?" she asks in a half whisper.

"Of course," he says, although this was not a possibility he'd thought about. With Tommy aboard it would not be quite the romantic adventure he'd envisioned. But Tommy could learn to sail, and a third hand on the boat would be valuable. He was prepared to make whatever compromises it took to have her come with him. Of that he was certain. "Tommy can sail with us as much as he wants," he tells her. "There are many reasons that would be a good thing."

He sees relief in her eyes.

She gestures toward the second letter lying on the table. "Ben's was much harder. I didn't know what to say to him that would make it any easier for him. That wouldn't hurt him more."

Before he can summon an appropriate response, she continues.

"All I could think to write was to apologize to him. And to thank him for all he'd done for me. For the years we had together. And for giving me Tommy."

"That sounds right," he says softly.

A fleeting frown crosses her face. "I don't know," she says. "I told him he's a good man. A decent man. I asked him to take care of Tommy. I said I loved them both and would miss them terribly. I hope that helps Ben, even a little."

Afraid of giving her false assurances about how Ben might react to her letter he says nothing. Only reaches across the table for her hand.

"When do we have to leave," she asks him abruptly.

He glances at his watch. "About three hours, allowing for preparation of *Shearwater*. And being at the entrance at the exact high tide."

"That's not much time," she says. "I need to repack that duffel. I assume suitcases aren't a good idea on a boat."

"Any soft pack is best."

"I'm thinking of leaving Toby here," she says, her eyes moistening again. "He's as much my son's cat as mine. And it might comfort Tommy to have him."

He nods. "The boat might not be best for Toby."

"I'll leave a lot of food and water for him now. They should be back today or tomorrow."

He sees tears at the edges of her eyes. "Are you going to be all right, Charlotte?"

She blinks hard. "I think so," she says, slowly.

He squeezes her hand and rises from the table. "I should get the boat ready. I'll come back for you in two hours. Will that work?"

She nods. "I'll be ready."

He comes around the table and pulls her up from the chair and caresses her face. "You won't regret this," he whispers. "I'll make you happy."

"I'm sure you're right," she says.

Charlotte

After he's gone, she's unable to find the energy to do what needs doing. She had so little sleep last night, and writing the letters drained her completely. Finally, she rises from the table and puts out food and water sufficient for Toby for three days, then cleans his litter box. She holds the Siamese to her chest, feeling tears well in her eyes. "I have to go away, Toby," she whispers. "You'll be okay. Tommy will take care of you." Her throat closes as she sets him down on the chair.

Now she finds strength to bring the duffel she packed for the storm to her bedroom. She unpacks it completely, being careful with the narwal, setting it on top of the dresser, to be carefully re-packed later.

She tries to think about what she should take with her. Nothing fancy. *How many things do you need to sail the world on a forty-foot ketch?* Not much, she tells herself. On the boat, space will be at a premium, and Michael will have to share with her.

She lays out sets of clothing, ranging from summer wear for the hot tropics to winter wear for Alaska and the Southern Ocean. She packs each item as tightly as she can in the duffel or her backpack. Then she adds a minimum of toiletries, half the money she and Ben keep in a coffee can in the kitchen, and her own checkbook. She finds her passport, which she's faithfully renewed each time it's expired since she went to Europe with her dad. When she's finished, she wraps the scrimshaw narwal inside a sweatshirt and places it in the middle of her backpack.

What she's packed is so little, compared to the dressers and closets still filled with her clothes and shoes and hats. She won't need all that. Ben can give it away. Whatever else she might require after spending time cruising, she can find it in the next major port they stop at. Michael will care for her. She believes his promise.

She looks at the clock on the end table. Almost two hours have passed already. *He'll be waiting at the dock*. Pulling on her pack, she lifts the duffel and gives a final glance at the bed she and Ben have slept in for more than a decade. "I'm sorry, Ben," she whispers to no one. Then she goes down the stairs, out onto the front porch and down the path to the dock, leaving the two letters on the kitchen table.

Michael is waiting for her, the inflatable tied to the dock.

"You have everything?" he asks.

"As much as I could fit in here," she says, handing down the duffel. She slides the pack off her shoulder and hands him that too.

He reaches a hand up to help her into the inflatable. That's when the panic attack hits. She freezes. Right there on the dock, with Michael's hand outstretched to her. She turns to stone.

She sees him waiting while tiny waves glitter in the sunlight behind him.

As she remains rooted to the dock, his eyes darken. Some terrible premonitions of disaster, she thinks.

Fear and doubt churn through her.

A long silence, only the cries of gulls squabbling on the beach.

Then his deep voice, tinged with encouragement. "You can do this, Charlotte."

She feels dizzy, realizes how little she's eaten today, with almost no sleep last night. *Fatigue makes cowards of us all.* She heard or read that once but can't remember where.

The emotions running through her are chaotic. She feels a desperate need to get her arms around them, but she doesn't know how.

Michael's hand is still stretched out to her, but she can't grasp it. She's fixed to the dock like a statue, or a celluloid film that breaks, leaving only one frame projected on the screen.

She's crying now. Through her tears she sees Michael's face darken even more. Then he climbs out of the inflatable onto the dock and holds her. But when he kisses her this time, she feels the grip of her sadness tighten around her heart. She can't breathe.

She tries to speak but finds no words.

He continues to hold her, but now his eyes are glistening too.

"I thought I could." She forces the words out.

He looks at her, a great sadness written across his face.

"But now I can't," she tells him.

He lets her go and leans down to take the pack and duffel from the dinghy. Then sets them carefully on the dock.

"I'm sorry, Michael," she says, sobbing.

"I understand," he whispers.

Now she grabs onto him, so tightly her knuckles turn white.

"I have to go, Charlotte. I have no choice," he says in a hoarse voice.

"I know," she says, letting go of him.

For a few moments neither of them moves, until he lowers himself into the inflatable and turns to her. "I'll wait a month in Port Townsend," he tells her. "Give you time to work things out with Ben and Tommy."

She nods. "Okay."

"I'll be at the Thatcher Marina. It's a small marina. You won't have trouble finding me there. If you don't come in a month…" his voice trails off.

He climbs out of the inflatable onto the dock and wraps his arms around her one last time.

She clings to him and whispers, "I love you, Michael."

" With my whole being I love you, Charlotte," he says, his voice breaking.

She lets go.

In the inflatable again, he starts the outboard and casts off.

She watches as he points the bow away from the dock.

Out toward where *Shearwater* lies.

Tugging at her anchor.

Michael

His hands are shaking as he motors out to his ketch. He feels as if the breath has been knocked out of him and sees himself—as if from an eagle's vantage—tiny and alone.

He wants to howl at the sky and scream at the sea. But he doesn't have time for that. Not even time to *think* about what's happened if he's to bring his ketch safely across the reef only minutes from now. Somehow for this moment, he must put aside his breaking heart and prepare *Shearwater* for leaving.

All morning the tide flooded into Eagle Cove, the water lapping higher and higher on the pebble and rock beaches. He glances at his watch and sees that the highest tide of the month will occur in just sixteen minutes.

Hurriedly, he ties the inflatable to a cleat at the stern and climbs the transom ladder. Orion rushes to greet him, tail wagging, eager for a head rub. Michael bends down to his Husky, forced to see him as his only companion again, and clutches the dog to his chest, his tears falling onto the Siberian's thick fur. Orion licks his face, sensing his sadness and turmoil.

Earlier, while Charlotte was packing, he'd hanked on the light air sails and properly stowed everything below. She'd let him fill the yellow five-gallon diesel container again from Ben's tank. More than enough fuel to raise the anchor and power out through the narrow entrance and onto the sea. Once free of Eagle Cove, he will raise the sails. *Shearwater* will be in her element again.

Now he starts the diesel and gives a bit of throttle.

Shearwater begins moving forward as he goes to the bow and cranks in the anchor line. When he feels the anchor break free, he brings it up and secures it in the bow chock.

As he comes aft down the side deck, he can't help but glance across the water toward the house. He sees Charlotte on the front porch watching him. She waves to him. He waves back, two arms over his head.

In the cockpit he faces forward, takes the wheel, and gives the engine more throttle. *Shearwater* gathers way. He points her bow to the middle of the cove's opening. He feels a great temptation to turn and wave once more. He forces himself not to look back. His heart is heavy.

He gives the diesel still more throttle, and now *Shearwater* drives ahead toward the high tide.

Towards an open, indifferent sea.

Charlotte

On the front porch, watching Michael leaving, she wonders how she could be this foolish, to let go of a man she loves like no other. She can't fathom it. Yet, she also can't understand how she believed it would be possible to leave Tommy and, even Ben. She'd tricked herself. Thinking she could walk away. But has she just passed up her only chance for a life in the larger world? For a true love. She brings a fist down hard on the porch railing. *I'm going mad with these contradictions.*

She lifts the pack and duffel from where she dropped them on the porch. Her heart is filled with ice. Watching *Shearwater* motoring toward the entrance, she can hardly breathe. She turns away and carries her belongings into the house and puts them behind the door in the catch-all room where Ben seldom goes. She'll find time later to unpack them and then hide the narwhal.

In the kitchen, she takes her letters to Ben and Tommy from the table, places them in the wood stove, and watches as they catch fire from still smoldering coals. She waits until the pages turn to ash and then goes into the downstairs bathroom.

When she looks in the mirror, she doesn't recognize herself. Her face is drawn, dark circles under her eyes, her hair disheveled. She feels sick, afraid she's losing her mind, bedeviled at having to choose between two men she loves differently, with her son in the balance.

She stares into the mirror, gripped by despair. She turns away from herself and stumbles down the hall to her sewing room. Her mother's Singer sewing machine glares at her, reminding her again of Michael hunched over it, sewing the red *Shearwater* spinnaker. How long ago that seems now, and how joyful then.

In the sewing drawer, she finds the large scissors for heavy fabric. Standing in front of the tall mirror on the back of the door, she reaches behind her and corrals the long sweep of her hair. "Damn you, Charlotte, damn you!"

In the mirror, she sees her right hand take the scissors and cut her hair only a few inches from her scalp. Thick strands of hair fall to the floor around her feet.

She watches in horrified fascination as the scissor cuts again. And again. And again. Until there's no more long hair to cut. She stares at this strange woman in the mirror, whose hair doesn't even reach her shoulders.

Now, she lowers her hand to her belly, rests it there. She doesn't understand how, but she knows with certainty she's pregnant. And that this short-haired woman, staring back at her, belongs with Michael Cordero on *Shearwater*. That's what this new woman knows and wants.

Dropping the scissors, she races down the hall, grabs a hat, then bursts out the front door, taking the porch steps two at a time, running madly down the path toward the dock. *Maybe I am mad.*

Shearwater is making way towards the entrance. She can see Michael standing at the helm. She shouts to him, "Michael! Michael! Wait!"

But she knows he's already too far away to hear her over the drone of his diesel engine. She waves her arms over her head as she runs, but he doesn't turn around.

At the dock, her fingers fumble with the lines holding the skiff. It seems to take forever to untie them. Climbing down, she presses the starter button for the outboard. The engine sputters, coughs, and dies. "For the love of God!"

Her heart hammers as she presses the starter again. This time, the engine catches and runs. She gives it full throttle, gunning the skiff towards the entrance, and *Shearwater's* retreating hull.

Within minutes she closes half the distance to the ketch. But Michael still has not turned around, and *Shearwater* is over the entrance reef now, she's certain of it. *Shearwater* has escaped. *Michael was right about the highest tide.*

Only a hundred yards behind the ketch now, the skiff is closing fast, and her heart beats wildly at the prospect of surprising him. She can see him standing at *Shearwater's* wheel, the wind blowing his hair, and she imagines his elation at seeing her, his smile that she loves —the upturned corners of his lips.

She turns her head slightly and sees another boat appear around the north bluff at the entrance. It takes her a minute to comprehend what she's seeing. But there it is, the *Emerald Rose.* And waving to her from the bow is Tommy.

In the narrow entrance *Shearwater* and the *Emerald Rose* pass within twenty yards of each other, then quickly draw apart.

"Mom, Mom!" Tommy shouts across the water. "What are you doing out here?Did you know we were coming home just now?"

The sound of her son's beautiful voice.

"Mom!" he shouts again. "You should see the salmon I caught."

She can't breathe. She turns down the throttle, and the skiff slows.

She glances towards *Shearwater* just as the ketch disappears around the south bluff. Then she turns her gaze back to Tommy.

He waves again.

She turns the skiff's bow towards the *Emerald Rose*.

Toward her son. And her husband.

Michael

As *Shearwater* draws away from Cambria Island, her sails fill with a fifteen-knot breeze, and she heels and drives forward. At any other time, Michael would revel at being on the sea again, free to sail after being trapped at anchor for nine days. But now he feels only sadness.

Above the island and Keller Peak, the sun's orange glow creates a halo—streaks of tenuous pink light reaching up toward the heavens like fingers. He takes this as an omen. Locking the wheel, he sets a course south, toward the Strait of Juan de Fuca and Port Townsend. He goes below and lifts the chart table cover and removes the plastic container in which he keeps his valuables. He'd put her locket in there, unwilling to carry it in his jeans while he's sailing—afraid he might damage it, or worse, lose it.

He opens the locket and for long minutes studies Charlotte's tiny photograph, holding it close to his eyes to see it better. Then he forces himself to return the locket to its place inside the chart table and goes back out to the cockpit.

While he was below, the orange and pink brilliance drained from the sky and a pearl glow illuminates the bottoms of distant clouds. Ahead, the flat water stretches away like a wide dark tongue, devoid of light. The sea lies deserted, an aqueous desert.

He's confronted now by the ocean's emptiness—its solitude and indifference. For the first time since he began sailing, the sea arouses an awareness of his estrangement from others. Charlotte has ruined solitude for him, he thinks. Now, not even Orion's familiar shape on the lazarette can dispel the dread he feels, that she won't come to join him in Port Townsend.

In such a short time he'd grown accustomed to her presence on board. The boat is permeated with the scents and remembered sounds of her. He longs for her to be at the helm.

As he stands at the wheel, the sky darkens gradually into shades of purple and finally blackness. The appearance of stars, winking and brilliant, makes him glance eastward, where an orange moon tears loose from the horizon and rises in the sky. He remembers moonlight streaming into the main cabin as they made love. If he turns, she would be here, moon-glow shimmering in her long hair. But when he looks, there's only Orion's dark form, silhouetted against silver light cast on the sea.

He shivers from the cold evening air that lays heavy on the silent channel. The shapes of the islands on either side seem only half real, and ghostly. Without Charlotte, the Sound feels strange and disturbing. He wonders again at the fates that brought him to Cambria Island. During the nine days *Shearwater* lay trapped in Eagle Cove, her hold over him had steadily advanced, like the tide creeping in when your back is turned, leaving you stranded on an offshore rock.

Over the last three days, with the terror of the storm and their shared courage in facing disaster, he thought he'd grafted her to him. Now he feels he might have misjudged the depth of her feelings. She'd been swept up in the passion of the moment. When that moment ended, she returned to the life she had.

Yellow phosphorescence glows in the water now, a spectral veil, trailing behind the sloop like the train of a wedding dress.

He'd allowed himself to imagine a life with her. It was easy to have such dreams.

He saw them sharing books and creating space for her painting. Dancing in the cool evening air. Sharing meals.

But now, he thinks, none of that will happen. Her joy as she stood at the ketch's wheel, her passion towards him on *Shearwater* and Keller Peak, seem like illusions—already slipping from his grasp.

He raises his eyes to the moon's shining face. Surely, the love he feels for her is enough to change her mind—enough to turn her heart to him—despite all that Ben and Tommy mean to her.

He clings to the wheel and struggles to convince himself she might still follow him to Port Townsend. Might choose what they would have together. That her love for him will triumph.

The dark water shimmers with the moon's mystery.

Within a month, he will know her answer.

Acknowledgements

I'm deeply indebted to the members of my two writing groups who made important contributions to this novel. From the "UCLA" group, Alicia Elkort applied her remarkable poetic sensibilities to raise the novel to another whole level of lyricism and flow. Eileen Heyes was the sharpest editing eye and fact checker for every draft, while Bill Sharpsteen applied his analytical skills to good effect. The "LA" group—Brandon Reim, Dawn Fratini, and Karen Sampson—contributed passion and endless imagination to make the characters and story more cinematic and vibrant. Thanks also go to my "beta" readers, Judy Winer, Charmaine Craig, Jennifer Flowers, Dorothy Pittman, Joan Friedman, Ben and Debbie McLeod, Ruthann Reim, Steve Emmes, and Eric Paerels for their valuable suggestions and enthusiastic support. I thank Ingemar Anderson of Kitsap Publishing for acquiring the novel, and for his patience and skill in guiding me through the process from manuscript to finished book. Finally, I'm indebted to the incredible beauty of Orcas Island, the Salish Sea, and the Inside Passage of British Columbia as seen from the deck of a sailboat, for inspiring the settings in this novel.

Acknowledgements

I'm deeply indebted to the members of my two writing groups who made important contributions to this novel. From the "LaLEA" group, Alicia Elliott applied her remarkable poetic sensibilities to raise the novel to another whole level of precision and flow. Eileen Hayes was the sharpest editing eye and fact checker for every draft, while Bill Sharpsteen applied his analytical skills to good effect. The "Lit" group—Brandon Reim, Divya Frajput, and Karen Simpson—contributed passion and endless imagination to make the characters and story more coherent and vibrant. Thanks also go to my "beta" readers: Judy Wine, Charmaine Craig, Jennifer Flowers, Dorothy Pittman, Jean Friedman, Pam and Debbie Sacred, Rayburn Reim, Steve Fortunes, and Eric Daniels for their valuable suggestions and enthusiastic support. I thank Ingemar Anderson of Kitsap Publishing for acquiring the novel and for his patience and skill in guiding me through the process from manuscript to finished book. Finally I'm indebted to the incredible beauty of Orcas Island, the Salish Sea, and the Inside Passage of British Columbia as seen from the deck of a sailboat, for inspiring the settings in this novel.

Printed in the USA
CPSIA information can be obtained
at www.ICGtesting.com
CBHW021137190524
8785CB00036B/615

9 781952 685705